TO WAKE A DRAGON

VENYS NEEDS MEN

NAOMI LUCAS

BLURB

It's been eight years since the red comet flew across our skies. Eight years since the blood moon. No dragon has been seen or heard from since.

Until now.

As one of the guardians of my tribe, I'm known as Milaye, a Protector of the Mermaid Coast. I've never had the honor of consideration as a future matriarch or a match for one of the rare males born near the Forbidden Jungle. I've kept my wishes hidden—despite my envy for my fellow tribemates who are happily mated.

I've lost hope for such a life long ago.

But one day, my ward flees into a long lost cave deep beneath the jungle brush. A cave, I soon realize, that holds a long-dead giant monster.

A *dragon.*

But he isn't really dead after all...

VENYS
Land of the Comet
Frozen Coast
White Wastes
Mist Lake
The Endless Forest
North Plains
Gulf of Mermaids
Flame Pass
Middle Plains
Sand's Hunters
Titan
Shell Rock
Titan's Tears
World Wall
Forbidden Jungle
Ember Pass
Giant's Steppes
Shimmering Peaks
Forsaken Sands
Golden Coast
Endless Blue Ocean
World's End
Map by NAOMI LUCAS

1

HAIME FINDS A CAVE

"Haime! Don't climb so high!" I yell.

I watch as my little ward claws her way up a jungle tree. She is seven seasons now, and I can scarcely believe how much time has flown by. It's been two years since she's been mine to train. Someday she will be a great huntress, and I've been honored with the duty to lead her down that path.

"It's all right, Auntie Milly. This tree is no match for me!" she shouts.

Indeed, it's no match for her. Haime is part-dragon. Part-dragon because her father, Zaeyr, turned into a human male during the red comet and mated with my clan-sister, Aida. Haime is the oldest of their four children, the eldest to a sister and two brothers. Together they've become the ruling family of Sand's Hunters—what with Zaeyr's might and Aida's gift to bear strong sons.

But only Haime has been given to me to train. Her sister, Edenth, just turned five seasons and already prefers healing and caretaking more than hunting and exploring. Edenth will apprentice with another.

Which is okay—because Haime is a handful. I adore her

though, maybe even because of it. She's like the daughter I have always wanted.

Since Aida gave her to me to train, Haime's filled a void in my heart. And I know why Aida gave her to me. She knows I love Haime dearly and would do all in my power to protect her, to train her into the fierce huntress she is destined to be.

I will never have a baby of my own. There are no males left for me. And...

Frowning, pushing away the thoughts that threaten to distract me, I follow Haime's shadow. She's moving through the leaves and up toward a higher branch. She and I are within the northern jungle, where the cliffs and lagoons of the south turn to long patches of giant plants and sand dunes. The trees aren't as thick here, but it's because the soil is drier. The jungle is also not as dark, nor as vibrantly green.

It's easier to track prey here.

The northern jungle eventually meets the middle plains of Venys, and the soil only gets drier from there. Other tribes rule those lands with their own laws, and unless necessary, we don't venture there.

But still, the north is a good place to train the young huntresses and not only because it's easier to track. Smaller creatures roam here, and I don't have to worry about ambushes from gorillas or jungle cats. Besides the occasional dune worm, cockatrice, or crocodile, there is not much to worry about.

And the sky is visible at all times, unlike the southern terra of the jungle, where the trees are thick and vines web throughout the canopy. The sky is often hidden because of the foliage. Knowing where the sun lies helps with telling time, and knowing the time helps with managing younglings.

"Haime, come down this instant!" I shout. "We must head back."

"I'm almost to the top," she cries. "I'm strong, remember? I will not fall."

Strong? Sure. But Haime's a child, and even with her dragon blood, she does not have the power of an adult, not yet.

"Oh!" she gasps.

Nervously, I debate going after her. "Oh? What do you see?"

"You were right, Auntie Milly! There's a storm coming in from the ocean."

A boom of thunder sounds the air, clamoring as if provoked.

Great. I roll my eyes. "I told you I heard thunder. Now get down here so we can make it back to the tribe in time."

Haime lands in front of me, startling me backward. *She jumped from the top of the tree.* My eyes widen in horror. The little imp grins upon seeing my expression—and I know it looks horrified, for I feel the horror all over.

I clutch her to me. "You could've hurt yourself," I shout, peering up at the tree. *So tall.* "Oh, waters, little dragon, don't ever do that again!"

Haime embraces me back. "I'm strong."

"It doesn't matter!" I pull back to cup her cheeks. "What would your parents think if I bring you back to the tribe with broken legs?" Simply imagining it sends a gruesome shiver down my spine.

"I would never do that to you, Auntie Milly."

Pressing her closer to me, despite knowing she's safe, my heart still pounds ferociously. "You'd better not. I couldn't live with myself after. I could not live knowing I had failed you and your parents. You may not be of my blood, but you are still mine, Haime."

Haime rests her little head on my chest and hums. It calms me. Her humming always calms me. Several minutes pass before I'm settled enough to let her go. Not even a pack of territorial apes could've forced me to release her sooner. She is the closest I will have to a child of my own.

But that is a pain I refuse to wallow in anymore. It's been

eight years since new males have joined my tribe, and both were mated to other, younger women: Aida and her sister, Delina. And since I was four years older than Aida, I would never be considered as a mate for a new male. But that wasn't the case eight years ago... Dragon males bonded with the one who turns them human.

Only one human male came to us eight years ago—from Shell Rock. Leith. The elders paired him with Delina.

The other two were dragon males, and they do not abide by the law of the elders.

Zaeyr, was once a great and ancient water dragon that ruled the waters of the Mermaid Gulf. The cursed red comet flew through the sky then, bringing out a mating heat in beasts across the land. Because of that heat, Zaeyr rose from the waters and bonded with Aida through an accident—and maybe fate—on the sands below the tribe.

When she touched him to protect our tribe, he lost his immortality and became human. Well, mostly human. Zaeyr still has scales, a tail, strange eyes, and claws. His children, like Haime, inherited many of his dragon features.

The other dragon male, Kaos, mated with a female from our neighbor tribe.

Their appearance renewed hope amongst the females of Sand's Hunters, and with that hope, many left the safety of our tribe to hunt down a dragon of their own. Myself included.

I hold in my breath thinking of that time. Like my clan-sisters, I never found a dragon of my own, and as the red comet faded from the sky, hope faded too. And so my search for a male quickly turned into rescue missions, searching for sisters who did not return. Some are still missing to this day, and recalling that time leaves a sour taste in my mouth.

We gained and lost so much.

Haime's humming returns, and I know she perceives my sadness. I force a smile to my lips. "Shall we make our way home?" I ask her. "I can't imagine you'd like to make camp out here during a rainstorm? There will be no fire to sit by and warm your scales."

She gives me a face. "No! Let's go. I want Aunt Delina's spicy fish."

"Promise you won't climb any more trees?"

"I promise," she whines.

I hand back her spear, shortened for her height. "Good. I'll let you lead, and I'll take point at your back." Excitement brightens Haime's face when I tell her this.

"Really?"

"Remember to watch out for quicksand pits, tracks, and spiderwebs," I remind her, putting my hands on her shoulders and turning her around.

Haime grasps her spear in both hands, stepping away. "Yes, yes!" She looks at me over her shoulder. "I will get us home safely, Auntie Milly."

My smile grows. "I know you will. Listen to the trees and the sounds of the jungle. And no running!" I yell, but she's already skipping away. "Don't forget to check above for snakes and cats!"

My ears ring with her laughter as she vanishes into the brush. Glancing once more at the tree, I expel the last of my worry and take off after her.

We walk for a while, and I point out tracks and plants as we go. Though we're trying to make good time, I can't pass up a teaching opportunity. Under my instruction, Haime forages the Lulia Moss we come across. It makes an excellent tea. I also show her an old cockatrice nest we stumble upon, the mother and chicks having long departed. Haime takes a cracked egg and stores it in her satchel to show her sister later.

The darkening sky doesn't deter us... yet. Neither do the squawking birds that rise from the trees and fly inland, nor the ever-increasing thunder. Scanning the jungle, it comforts me to find thick tangles of vines. I know these trees like I know my ability to take down the prey that resides within them.

"Milly," Haime calls as she steps over a log. "How close do you think we are from home?"

"Why don't you guess?"

"I can't tell when we're in the jungle! Can't we head to the shore?"

"No. I told you that the crocodiles are breeding—" A low hissing sound cuts me off. "Haime, don't move!"

She stops, turning to me.

I hold my finger to my lips and her little eyes go wide. The hissing gets louder, as I shift my spear to my right hand and slowly pull the dagger from my belt. Haime takes a step toward me as I quietly move to her side. She gently sets down her satchel and brandishes her smaller spear.

"It's a naga," I tell her. Nagas roam the Forbidden Jungle and are perilous when cornered. They're worse if they have eggs nearby, for then they set up defenses to protect themselves and their nesting grounds. But this wasn't a nesting ground. I'm sure of it. I only hear one hiss amongst the foliage.

"Not a snake?" Haime whispers.

"Listen to the inflection. It's deep, raspy. Snakes don't sound like that." The hissing is close by and getting closer, coming from a grouping of large bushes ahead of us. I motion for Haime to keep backing up until she's behind me. The leaves rustle, and I brace for the naga's appearance. Highly intelligent —debatably even sentient—an adult naga could sometimes be reasoned with. With an offering of meat. "If it attacks, Haime, I want you to run. Understand?"

"I can help," she whines.

"No, not against an adult."

"But—"

"No buts."

The rustling grows louder, and Haime falls silent. Twigs

snap, and a frog scurries out from under the bush. I'm holding my breath as the branches part and the gleam of dark eyes appears between the leaves. Solid black, they stare at us. *They're small*, I realize, my brow furrowing.

The hissing heightens, and the bush shifts to reveal the naga entirely—a youngling. A male youngling, due to the lack of breasts. His tail slides forward and lashes out in warning. There's fear etched across the boy's dirty face.

I lower my weapon. "Are you alone, little one?"

He bares his teeth and snaps at me.

I take a step forward, free palm extended, disarming. "It's okay," I coo. Peering about, I don't find any sign of adult nagas with him.

"Milly, what's going on? Is... is he okay?" Haime says.

"I don't know. Just stay back." I focus on the boy, who's pressed farther into the brush but still watching us—watching Haime. I shouldn't try to help him, but he's a child, no older than her, and even if he is a naga, it hurts my heart to think he's all alone.

"Can we help him?" Haime asks.

Without answering, I put my dagger away and reach out to the boy. "It's okay," I say again. "You're okay. We won't hurt you." Yet I know he could still *hurt* us.

His eyes shift to me, and he hisses loudly. I take another small step forward. There is now a softness to his gaze. Perhaps he will calm—but thunder sounds and he startles.

"No!" I cry as he slips into the bushes and vanishes.

"Wait!" Haime runs past me and dives into the brush.

"Haime. Stop!" But she's already crashing through the plants ahead. I take after her as the first raindrops fall from above. "Haime! Don't!" She doesn't listen, doesn't stop. My eyes dart every which way, searching everywhere for her trail.

"Please wait!" She calls out ahead.

"Haime!"

Soon after the noise of pursuit stops and my trail goes dead. I scream for Haime, but she doesn't answer, my only response to the *whoosh* of rain falling upon the leaves around me. *No, no, no.* Backtracking, I search for signs of a trail but am only led back to the thick clearing of grass and brush, the place where I'd lost my ward.

Heart hammering, I yell for Haime again, my panic increasing by the second, turning full-circle. I swipe out my spear to push back the overgrown leaves and vines. I beg for any clue to where she's gone. My sandals begin to stick as mud gathers at my feet. *Soon, any tracks will vanish.*

The storm will wipe her trail clean.

I scream louder, desperate for a response. I pivot again when I see it—a large cropping of mossy rocks, tucked between arching roots from a nearby tree. But it's not the rocks that pull my attention, it's the ancient remnants of a naga nest and the pit in the ground behind it, hidden between the rocks. I surge forward and crouch at the pit's entrance. *Has she fallen? Was the boy bait?*

"Haime!" I shout inside it. *It's deep*, I realize, ducking in. *Deeper than just a pit.* It's a hole—a cave entrance.

"Milaye," Haime calls back to me, her voice muffled from somewhere deep within. A wave of relief crashes through me. I've found her.

"Haime, are you okay!? Are you hurt?"

"The boy ran in here, but I can't find him—I can't see." Her high-pitched cry is far off. "I can't see. I can't see!" It grows shrill.

"Stay right there. I'm coming after you!" Setting my spear aside and pulling away from the entrance, I search for a piece of wood to light, but the rain has made its way down to drop in splats upon the underbrush. Rushing to the old naga nest, I find broken branches, concealed under the tree's large roots. Grabbing the biggest of the branches, I tug out flint and fire moss from my pouch. By rubbing the moss at the end of the branch, I make a crude torch.

Returning to the cave opening, I light the torch and drop to a crouch. "I'm coming," I call out. "Don't move!"

Holding the torch before me, I unsheathe my dagger and descend into the cold darkness.

2

DRAZAK'S DREAM

Petrichor invades my mind. The scent of fresh rain in the air, and the feel of that rain upon my wings. It slides over my muscles and between my scales, and with it is the smell of soil. Rich soil, filled with minerals and dampened with water. It calls to me like a flame in the darkness and brings me peace.

I am familiar with this dreamy feeling. It is one I have had countless times. So many times that the memories blend together until my life is one reverie after another. I also know somewhere, not here, it is real and more than a pleasant feeling.

It is raining.

My body does nothing with this knowledge, and I settle into it. I have tried and tried to hold onto more than these feelings —they only serve as a reminder of the passing of time—to no avail. It is the rain that keeps me sane... I think. It is the rain, the soil, and the damp all around me that has given me the knowledge of time. I have gone through this thousands of times, and because of that, I know I have lain here for hundreds of years.

I think.

So, I have settled into this cursed life, and I wait until the day that I finally fall into true darkness from which I will not wake up again.

Venom runs through my veins, poison, paralyzing me. An enormous injection that should have killed me long ago. Except I am an alpha dark dragon, and my body's strength fights back death, even if I wish for it. Death does not come easy to dragons —especially dark dragons. We are resistant to it. And herein lies the humor...

What makes me powerful and mighty has also cursed me.

My heart pulses hard at the thought.

The only satisfaction I have is that the poison dragon who bit me is dead. I made sure of it before I fell from the sky and crawled into this cave, planning to recover—*HAH!* I tore off that dragon's head with my teeth, forcing his body down to the world as I fell. His taste still lingers in my mouth, rancid and bitter. The memory of his blood spraying across my body comforts me when insanity threatens, replacing it with glee.

He did not take my territory.

That is all that matters. Though sometimes I wish he had. Then perhaps my rage would give me the motivation to rise again, to tear him to shreds.

He wanted to steal my nest.

My territory is in a prime location... With the gulf nearby and the fertile jungle filled with creatures large enough to eat, hunger was never a worry. And with its central location, the likelihood of a femdragon in heat flying by was high.

Fellow dragons envied my territory.

Though whether it is still mine, I do not know. I sense other alphas now and again, but I do not know if they sense me. It is not like the rain. Alphas do not approach one another unless they are of the same blood or fighting over territory—or a mate. One has never sought me out, and so I believe my presence goes unnoticed. Surely, if one had, they would kill me and put me to rest.

"Wait! Stop!"

My heart weakly thumps again. *Is that a voice? No. The only voices I hear are in my head. Drazak, fight the insanity.*

"Wait!"

I hear it again. It is muffled though, as if it is coming from a distance. The voice does not sound like my thoughts, but I cannot be certain. I no longer know if I can distinguish outside sounds from those within my body.

But then I hear it again. "Don't run!" It is closer—and this time, there is a hissing sound. I have heard this hissing many times recently. It is not a sound I enjoy. It is soon followed by other noises though, the sound of scurrying and frantic movements.

Something cold brushes the side of my tail, but then it is gone.

Drazak, you have gone mad.

"Haime... Haime!" Another voice shouts.

It is a deeper voice than the first but not by much. Are there two beings sharing my head with me? They are speaking with each other now, and the worst part, it is in tongues. They are not speaking my language.

I have never wished for the darkness more than I do now.

Though one of the voices intrigues me. The second, deeper one. It is distinctly feminine. *Why would a female's voice be in my head?* My ever-present frustration intensifies.

Darkness take me!

If I am to be cursed with the allure of a female, then I would rather be dead. She is not real, and worse yet, I cannot understand her. I have done nothing but *want* for eons. Want for control. Want for dominion. Want for vengeance. But this? This would be torture. I have so far been blessed with never scenting a femdragon's heat in my cave, and the thought of that happening when I am powerless... horrifies me.

Before I fell, I wanted a mate and dragonlings. To want them again, and still be denied, would be a terrible kind of torture, the type I do not know I could endure.

There is a reason I fought so hard for my territory. It was not only for my pride and its location, but it was for the hope that a femdragon in heat would someday fly by and call out. I was preparing a nest... A nest I never finished but am lying in anyway. At least I know now that it is safe.

"Stay right there. I'm coming for you!"

My heart pulses with anticipation.

It is getting closer, louder.

Hope blasts through me that this, these sounds, may bring me my salvation.

3

—————

MILAYE IN THE DARK

I CRAWL through dead leaves and roots before the tunnel opens up enough for me to stand. Dirt sticks to my skin from where the rain has wetted me, and I silently curse Haime's recklessness.

The fact that she can't see bothers me. *She's always been able to find her way in the dark... It's those dragon eyes.* I brush off my misgivings, persuading myself it's only because she's deep in a cave.

She's my life but will be the death of me, I'm sure of it. But for now, I'm thankful, from the waters to the clouds and back, because I found her. Finding her safe—and ensuring she remains that way, despite her attempts to the contrary—is all that matters.

"Milly?" I hear her up ahead. "W-where are you?"

I lick my lips. "I'm almost there," I call out to her.

Waving my torch before me, the dirt tunnel has been replaced by a tight, rocky path. It's claustrophobic and makes me antsy—especially since my spear remains outside—but I take it as a good sign that Haime is okay.

If she'd fallen into a pit...

I don't even want to finish the thought. There are many caves along the coast, and some are just deep holes. My tribe stays clear of them because crawling out can be a rigorous ordeal.

Still... A strange cave is not the place a huntress wants to be. I survey the walls around me. You never know what could be dwelling within. I have to be ready for anything. There could be snakes, spiders, or worse, little naga children leading you into a trap. Gripping my dagger hard, I pray to the waters that isn't the case.

Hurting a youngling naga unnerves me, but if it's to protect Haime, I wouldn't hesitate.

Something scuttles over my foot, and I shriek, kicking out. It flies away, and I hop around, crying out with displeasure. Bumps prickle my skin, and I stick out my tongue in disgust. I hate bugs. *Bugs are the worst.*

Haime's going to clean fish for the next year after this. I shake out the feeling from my foot.

"Aunt Milaye, are you okay?" Haime yells.

No! No, I'm not okay! Bugs are never okay. My stomach churns. "Yes," I say though. *Just wait until I tell your mother.* Aida will make her clean all the fish in the village for years for this. I daydream of swimming in the springs and scrubbing my skin clean, and the thought keeps me moving forward.

Luckily the rock walls don't get any tighter, though I doubt the ease of passage is a good sign. It means something travels through here a lot, and I hope it's nothing more than the naga. But I don't hear any hissing. That assures me there are no traps, at least for now. Then the path diverges, coming to a fork, and I frown.

"Haime?"

"Milaye?" Her voice came from the right-hand path. It sounds clearer than ever, and I know she's near.

Eyeing the left path, I tug my satchel forward and root out

my bag of clamshells. I don't want to spend the time searching it—leaving Haime alone any longer—but I don't like having the trail at my back. Something could be lurking within. Instead, I sprinkle the clamshells on the ground. The thin shells aren't common, but this is not a waste; they make a great alarm if stepped on. Placing them around a campsite at night can be what saves you from a predator sneaking up while resting. The sound startles them, and you.

Moments later, I'm heading toward Haime, and the tightness in my chest eases when I hear her breathing.

"Watch out, there's a ledge," she says just as the tight walls enveloping me vanish and my torch illuminates a drop-off. Haime emerges below, blinking several times from the torchlight. The edge is steep and smooth, as if at one point, it'd been eroded by water.

Getting on my knees, I place the torch and dagger on the stone beside me.

"Are you okay?" I ask, reaching down.

"I think so…" Haime grasps my hand but lowers her head. "I'm sorry. Please don't be mad at me."

"Look at me," I order, waiting until she does. There's shame etched across her face, but I refuse to let it get to me. My lips flatten as I try to haul her up. She's resisting. "We'll talk about this once we're outside. An apology wouldn't have saved you if you'd been attacked, or if I hadn't found the hole." I try to lift her again. "Why aren't you helping me?"

Haime blinks at me. There's a sheen in her pupils. "The naga boy is down here."

I stiffen, and my free hand finds my dagger. Peering out into the darkness, I see nothing even with the halo of torchlight. I hear nothing but Haime. That doesn't mean there isn't something there though. "Where?" I ask.

"I don't know. I lost him. I was able to see until I came in here, and then something happened…"

"What happened?" I grip her harder. "Wait. Let's get out of here, then we'll talk." I don't like this. Haime can see well in the dark, but if she's as blind as I am right now... that's frightening. The dragon blood in her veins makes her different than any human. Despite her appearance, which makes her differences obvious, Haime is stronger, keener, and has sharper senses than any child I know.

I try to pull her up, but she resists me again. "Haime," I say her name in warning, edging closer to her. My hip bone bumps precariously against the ledge

"I can see again now there's light. I can't leave him."

"We have to *go*."

"But he's alone and hungry."

"You don't know that for sure. Come, the torch won't last forever, and it'll be harder to get out of here without it. Trekking through the jungle at night is far more dangerous, and we're running out of daylight."

"No!" She rips her hand from mine, pulling with such force I fall forward. "We can't leave him!"

A cry tears from my throat as I land, full frontal, on the cave floor below, partially on Haime herself. She's beneath me, crawling out from under me, crying, as shocked tears fill my eyes. With my arms shielding my face, I groan as Haime flips me over and climbs over me.

"Milaye? Milaye! I'm so sorry!" She shakes me ferociously, her childish voice heightened with fear. "Milly! Please get up."

My hands fall off my face and I moan, feeling the pain pulse through my arms, my knees.

"Milaye? We need to find the boy."

I moan again, trying to sit up. I press my palms to my brow, hard. "Nooo," I croak. She shuffles back from me. I slowly drop my hands down.

"We have too!"

"Haime..." My vision wavers.

I reach out for her, weakly, but she scoots back. Everything turns to a blur.

"Smells strange in here. It smells like hurt—pain. He's in pain," she whimpers.

"Haime. Don't," I beg weakly as I try to grab her, but she's no longer there. "Haime!" I shout as I hear her scurry off into the darkness. I nearly fall over but catch myself before I do. Worry careens through me. It was always there, even after I found her, but with the fall, I'm disoriented.

If something should attack, I'd be an easy target. *Get up.*

She's an easier target.

Get up!

I call Haime's name again as I rise to my feet. My toes curl with the effort, and I brace my palm against the rocky ledge to keep me from falling. Thank the waters for the torchlight above, it keeps me balanced.

When I'm certain nothing is broken, only bruised, I reach up, grabbing at the ledge until I find my dagger. With it back in my hand, I'm a little less scared.

Scared?

I can't believe it, but there's fear. I'm in a situation I'm not prepared for, and Haime's run off again. I wrench my eyes closed and shake my head before opening them, peering into the dark. Swallowing, I know I have to venture further into it.

Haime said she couldn't see without the light. I frown. Carefully, I stretch my body against the wall and nudge the handle of my makeshift torch toward the side. Once it's close enough, I roll it with the tips of my fingers until I can grip it. With it below, I'm able to see a little more of my surroundings. But Haime was right, it's so dark, like a black void where the light ends. There are no edges of rocks, roots, or walls. There's nothing outside my light. Nothing.

I'm already dizzy from the fall, but this... this is like being upended by a wave and not knowing which way is up to break the surface of the water. My breathing shallows.

Must find Haime.

I shake away my fear.

I can't punish her if I can't find her. And *waters*, is she in for some discipline. I hold onto the thought as I pull a feather out of my hair and lay it on the ground by the wall, a trail to help me find the way out later. I twist around and take a steadying breath.

I step into the vacuous, open cavern, and shiver.

4

DRAZAK'S FUROR

*H*AIME. *Haime. Haime.*

This strange word keeps repeating. I do not understand its meaning, but when I think it has finally stopped, I hear it again.

Is this it? Have I gone crazed?

Am I hearing voices, real or imaginary? It has been so long I cannot recall the sounds of the last voices I heard. Nor do I want to, knowing it was the poison dragon's taunts. His voice would send me into a rage.

Haime!

But this voice is not a dragon's. I am sure of it. And if it were, it must be a femdragon's, it's too sweet and lyrical to be a male. The likelihood of a femdragon being here, in this cave of all places, it is impossible. Femdragons keep to themselves far more than males, and though they prefer to travel—rarely claiming territory of their own—they only engage with others if they are in heat.

This femdragon will not save me. Even if she is more than a voice in my head.

I do not want to feel it—*this hope*—but it is there nevertheless.

What if? No... My heart thumps repeatedly.

This is not a femdragon.

But...

I have not felt this way, not since I fell from the sky and crawled into this cave, racing against time before the poison took its full effect. I have not endured this feeling of excitement even before then. It has been so long that I fear my mind might shatter. It hurts. I hurt.

"That girl," the feminine voice sours. So close now, almost too clear to be an illusion, and I am nearly wild with anticipation. "She's never leaving the tribe's rocks again if I have a say in it." It is like a mumble across my wings.

I wish I knew these words.

Have I been here so long that my kind's language has changed? The thought perturbs me. This whole situation frustrates me. Why is this happening now? That I cannot even seek out answers reignites my anger.

But the only part of me that moves is my heart. It beats despite everything. It is the one muscle not affected by the poison—which is stagnant deep within—and never has been. The slow thread of blood that pumps through me is what keeps me alive. *And the darkness...* I am certain my continued cursed life has lasted this long because of the darkness that feeds my body.

A strange scent fills the air, a beautiful, new scent, and I am transfixed. Hoping for change is one thing, hoping for death another, but hoping for a female is crazy.

This smell though... This is the smell of a female.

There is sweat and sea salt; there is jungle lily and spice. There's a twitching in my nostrils, expanding for these smells to enter me, and I am stunned.

I twitched.

My mind goes blank. I barely comprehend what is happening. Whatever it is, I do not want it to end. Life after this moment will be worse than all that has already happened to me. To breathe in the ocean and jungle after so long, only to have the sensation taken away...

Something small rams into my side. I hear a groan, and the sensation vanishes.

"To the waters and back, my foot!"

The voice and the smell are so close now that I am all but salivating. Something warm flares across my back leg, and a gasping noise sounds my ears.

All noise stops completely soon after, not even the quiet breaths or moans continue.

Do not go away. I plead. But something is happening at my hindleg, and I am unable to investigate. All I can do is wait.

Minutes pass by, and my heart only hammers harder. The bloom of heat returns along my foot but disappears soon after. Now it is at my tail.

It is fire, I realize. *Something is wielding fire beside me. Nothing can wield fire like this but another dragon or...*

No.

A human.

Horror rushes through me. A human has found me. A great alpha dark dragon—a rarity in the world I once knew—lying paralyzed as a human nears. And not just any human, a *female* human.

If she touches me, I lose everything. Everything that I have not already lost. My greatness, my majesty, even my hope that I will beat this poison—that I may one day fly.

I will die human, bonded to a female, left unable to mate as the breeding heat consumes me.

That would be cruel and painful and far worse than my sorry state now. I will lie here desperate for rutting, unable to either defend myself or take my female and dominate her, and as I grow crazed with lust, terrible shame will drown me.

How much more will I be forced to endure? My thoughts roar. *To be human and paralyzed...*

I do not want to die while losing my mind with mating heat. A female, even a human one, will not want a mate who cannot move. I am nothing if I cannot protect her.

She will be shamed for my shame.

I need to scare her away.

I tense, strain my muscles, but nothing happens. Not even the twitching of my nostrils builds into something more. The tap of human footsteps punctures the silence, and pressure strangles my insides. Furor fills me, replacing the annoyingly delectable human scent, and my mind continues to roar.

I will not be human, I bellow.

I will meet the darkness as the mighty beast I am.

5

____

A BIG, DEAD DRAGON

My foot aches, but it goes ignored as I stare at the—the giant monster before me. My breaths are shallow, my throat tight, and blood rushes from my face.

I want to scream for Haime, I want to run, but I do neither, waiting for the beast to rise and eat me whole. This wasn't just a forgotten cave—or a naga's nest—that Haime stumbled upon. It's a den.

A dragon's den.

My eyes water as I stare at the muscles and meaty curves of the beast. Minutes pass as my heart races, waiting for death, praying Haime is far away and hidden, when it occurs to me the dragon's crooked leg hasn't so much as twitched. The gleam of my torchlight glints, but the light does not shift upon its glistening scales.

It's not moving.

It's not even breathing.

Is it... is it dead?

As the thought takes over my mind, I remember what I'm staring at: a dragon. My back straightens, and my breathing eases. *If it tried to attack Haime or me, it would've done so by now, and if it had... all I had to do was touch it to save us.* That doesn't mean the beast isn't dangerous, but the realization gives me relief anyway.

Come to think of it, I could reach out and touch the dragon now. I'm not even an arm's length away.

I could claim it.

I frown, glancing down at my foot that had rammed into it, curling my aching toes. My sandal shielded my body, but even if it hadn't, would such a clumsy touch bond me and this dragon together?

I try to think back at all that happened to Aida when she encountered Zaeyr the first time. *She touched his wing.* Her touch had been deliberate.

Right?

Licking my lips, my eyes rove the shadowy mass. My skin prickles. It still hadn't made a noise, still hadn't moved, and the longer my thoughts whirl, the more I believe it has to be dead. Fate wouldn't bind me with a dead thing, would it? And the touch of my foot hadn't been deliberate, but then again, I don't think my skin made contact.

Did the skin need to make contact? My brows furrow. That was a question I didn't have an answer for.

I'm not even sure it's male, but what if it is...

I bite down on my tongue.

Why am I even thinking of this? I take a step back. The last eight years flash through my head. The pain, the want, the envy.

The red comet, the dragons, the very few males remaining in the tribes of the Mermaid Gulf. The days upon days, months upon months, years of wishing I would have a male of my own —a family of my own. I never cared about power or being a matriarch. I loved hunting and teaching the young daughters of Sand's Hunters how to protect themselves and provide for others—but I desperately always wanted one for myself. A daughter of my own. A little girl who would curl up under my arm, snuggling with me as we gazed upon the crackling fire in the safety of my hut.

A babe to hold against my chest and stare up at me with wide-eyed wonder. A beautiful child who I could call my own, that no one could ever take away from me. I never knew how badly I wanted to be a mother until I matured and began training the girls younger than me. Now, they are all older, huntresses themselves, and I'm enveloped with pride every time I see them.

But they go to their mothers when in need, not me.

No, consideration for the tribe matriarch and a mate were taken from me and my sisters when Aida and Delina were born. There were more males in their ancestry.

I swallow, staring at the giant hind leg of the dragon without really seeing it anymore. And it is a giant leg. Though laid out and crooked, the bend of the knee comes to my chest. I squeeze the handle of my dagger, distracting my hand.

I'm desperate to reach out and touch the beast. Eight years ago, I would've done so without hesitation.

My fingers shake.

What harm would it do if it's dead? A self-deprecating laugh runs through my mind. Everything I have always wanted is right before me, yet not.

Taking a step back, I move my torch around, trying to figure out how large the dragon really is instead. But the darkness is thick, and its body goes well above my head and into the cave ceiling. Cocking my head, I discover that the dragon has been here so long that the cave has partially formed atop it.

Maybe that's how it died?

How long has this creature been here? I pull my bottom lip into my mouth.

Carefully moving along its side, I follow its length, dazzled by its scales. They gleam deep purple and black—I have never seen colors of the like in the wild. I want to covet them. And strangely enough, it seems a deep, shadowy smoke emanates from them, dimming out my torchlight, but when I try to take a better look, the smoke dissipates, making me wonder if I'm seeing things. I shake my head and continue on.

There are spikes and long claws but I refuse to dwell on them. I want to see its face, look at it head-on, capture its mightiness in my mind so I can remember this forever. My heart bleeds, longing for this dragon to be mine—my mate—my lover.

My throat tightens.

Zaeyr, Aida's dragon, is the most virile and attractive male along the Mermaid Coast, only matched by Kaos, another dragon who lives in a neighboring tribe. But I can't help but imagine that this dragon—if human, if male—would put those two to shame.

He is mine. Even if he's dead, he will forever be mine. I squeeze my eyes shut but soon reopen them, knowing I can't linger.

Finally, I reach the dragon's neck, and my heart thunders. I'm almost to my destination. Enthralled. I'm enthralled. I've barely breathed and now stop altogether. Picking up my feet, I quicken my steps to the front.

The first thing I see is his very long snout, much longer than expected, and streaks of purple and black scales alight the dragon's features. My eyes glisten with them. They're like lightning at night, seen from the shore, a storm far off the coast. Following them from the snout, I lift my torch higher, catching a glimpse of the dragon's firmly shut eyes. They're huge, like the rest of him, but my focus doesn't linger, moving to the glassy jewel-like appendage between them, at the center of his forehead.

The giant deep purple stone captures my attention, and my lips part. Nearly as big as my head, a jewel I have never seen the likes of fills my vision. This time, I'm certain I see wisps of black coming off of it. Glancing down at the dragon's scales once more, I find the tendrils again.

I'm not seeing things.

Why would it be smoking? My gaze returns to the jewel. I sniff the air but smell nothing but dirt. Putting my dagger into my belt, I reach out to touch the jewel—

I stop short and snatch my hand to my chest.

"Milaye!"

Startling, I twist around. "Haime?"

What am I doing? I shake myself, dashing away from the dragon's corpse. I'd completely lost focus. *Anything could've snuck up on me—attacked me. I would've let them.* I'm never this absent-minded, especially in such a dangerous place.

"Milaye, say something again!"

Haime needs me. I hasten back to the direction I think I heard her from.

"Haime!" I yell. I come to the cave wall when something runs out of the shadows. It's heading straight for me. Tensing, I swing out my torch with a cry, but the figure stops short. Haime's features come into view, her arms outstretched.

Without pausing, I drop the light and fling my arms around her, pulling her hard to my chest.

"Stooop—" she whines, but I don't.

I lean down and bury my face into her hair. "You stupid, stupid girl. You could've gotten killed." Tears well in my eyes. "Never—and I mean never—run away from me again!"

Haime tries to tug free, but I grip harder. "He ran away," her voice is muffled by my chest.

"I don't care!" My frustration returns. I release her enough to hold her gaze. "You could've gotten yourself killed, or worse! He could've been bait to lead you into a trap. You could've been hurt! And you ran into a cave, *of all places!* A cave I had no idea existed. If I hadn't found it, what would you have done? Wander around in the dark and hope you found a way out?

That is *if* you didn't get hurt in the process? Do you know what kind of monsters makes their homes in caves? Some of the worst!"

The dragon's body comes to mind.

"I didn't know it was going to be so dark," Haime gripes.

"I don't care. You never do something like that. Ever!" I want to shake her, make her understand, but she's still a child, and ultimately it was me who failed her. I tug her back to me and wipe my tears away.

I'd never forgive myself if something had happened to her while I was preoccupied with the dragon. If something had happened to her at all.

"Promise me you won't do that again?"

She sighs, shoulders shrugging, like my question annoys her. "I promise."

"I mean it, seashell. I'll never take you out on a hunt again if you don't."

"I promise," she says again. "You won't tell Mama and Father, will you?"

"I am most definitely going to tell them."

"But—"

I let her go. "Just because you're sorry doesn't mean you didn't know better. This wasn't some mistake, Haime, you could've gotten us both killed. We will tell your parents and deal with the punishment, you and I both. That is what a Sand's Huntress does. We face all things with courage despite the situation. We make mistakes, and we own up to them."

"Yes, Milly."

I gaze at her for a moment longer, sucking my lips into my mouth before nodding. "Good. Then let's get out of here and go home." I grab the torch from the ground. "Stay close to me," I order.

"But what about the naga boy?"

I move around Haime, looking for the exit. "What about

him? We're not going after him, if that's what you're wondering."

"But he looked hurt and sickly! He might need food."

I frown, a little disoriented in the darkness. There's nothing around us but more darkness. "I know, but he's not ours to care for. He's a dangerous creature of the jungle, one that could sooner hurt us than accept our help, and from the looks of him, he didn't want our help. He wouldn't have run otherwise." Part of me fears running into the dragon with Haime in tow. It'll just dredge up old memories and wants again, and I don't want Haime to see it.

My gut churns at the thought.

Haime's half-dragon. I don't know what it would do to her if she saw one of her kind, and in such a state. There's no precedent for it. No one in the tribe—not even Haime's father—thought we'd encounter another dragon once the red comet left the sky.

But it wasn't only that, the dragon is *mine*. Something in me claimed him. It seems ridiculous but I felt that way. Like an invisible string attached itself from my soul to him.

"I thought a Sand's Hunter protector was always to help those in need," Haime argues.

"*Those,* meaning humans," I correct. "Nagas aren't human."

"My dad isn't human."

I stop and face her. "Haime, that's different. Your father is an intelligent creature, an ancient, and one able to bond with a human. He may not have been human once, but he is now. He is family."

Haime pouts.

"No more arguing. At this rate, we won't be back to the tribe until well after dark."

"Then we should camp here and maybe—"

"No."

I lead her further in the direction I think the exit is, but only darkness greets us. A chill dances across my skin. At first, the cave didn't seem like it would be so big, but now I'm not sure...

When we reach a rocky wall, I nearly sigh in relief, but soon realize there's no ledge above, and when I look down, my feather isn't there. I glance to either side, no idea which way to go.

"Haime, do you see anything nearby?" I ask.

She peers around. "Big shadows and rocks."

"What about the ledge we came in by?"

She shakes her head.

"Alright," I keep my voice calm. I pick a direction and follow it.

Haime tugs my hand. "There's something over there." She points ahead of us and slightly to the left. "I think I saw it when I was looking for the boy."

I inhale and nod. "Good." *Good.* Hopefully that means we're still close to the ledge, that we haven't accidentally gone deeper. I swear this cave seemed much smaller. I move us from the wall, in the direction Haime pointed.

"Why aren't my eyes adjusting?" Haime asks.

"I don't know. Perhaps it's how deep the cave is."

I recall the inky black smoke that came from the dragon's scales and jewel. *Could it be...?* I shake my head, pushing the thought away. I don't want to know if this darkness is something more than the absence of light.

"I can see in the caves near home."

I fail to respond. Something appears before us, glistening and filmy. It catches the flames, and glittering light purple streaks fill my vision. It takes me a moment to realize... it's part of the dragon's wing.

"What's that?"

I grab her and turn her away. "Nothing. It's nothing."

Waters, no. Please no. I try to lead us back the way we came.

But Haime tugs free and pushes past me. She rushes past the torch and I fling it away so it doesn't harm her. I lose my footing and trip.

"Milaye?" she cries, and I hear the horror in her voice as I fall.

Dizziness fills me. My heart drops into my stomach. I caught myself with my palms—but my hands aren't pressed against stone or dirt. I'm touching something smooth and silken. I look up to see Haime is touching the dragon too.

My fingers curl inward.

"It's a dragon!" I hear her scream.

My dragon.

Heat shoots up my arms.

6

BONDED

I'M FROZEN, staring at the purple sheen of wing under my hands. It twitches and then moves. My arms grow hot, burning, and I jerk back, grabbing my fallen torch and Haime at the same time.

It's alive.

I force Haime away, and for once, she doesn't fight me. But even though I'm no longer touching the dragon, the heat in me grows, expanding from my arms to my chest. A blast of air strikes us, sending our flames dancing. Something crashes nearby, and I grapple with Haime. Another crash, and then I hear it.

A low, echoing growl. It should've been lost among the falling rocks, but it's not. The growl fills my ears, and I'm pierced with another jolt of warmth.

Staggering, I drop my torch again and clutch my chest. My heart is on fire. In my haze of shock, Haime picks up our light —and a rock crashes beside us. We both jump.

"Milaye, it's waking up," Haime yells.

"Run!" I scream.

Our fingers intertwine, and we surge into the darkness.

Despite the warmth bursting through me, I search wildly for the ledge, desperate to find the exit as Haime waves the torch. She tugs me to the left just in time when another boulder falls. We dodge the impact and—I see my feather. It flutters on the ground.

I've never witnessed a more beautiful sight.

"Here!" Pulling Haime after me, I run to it, and the dark line of the ledge appears.

I waste no time and grab Haime's waist, lifting her. She drops the torch above and climbs up. A second later, she turns around, watching as I reach up and grab the ledge.

"Run! I'll be right behind you."

She hesitates. Tears are falling down her cheeks.

"Go!" I scream. "Don't wait for me!"

Dust litters the air, rocks are raining everywhere, but it's the growling roar that sends terror through my bones as it grows louder and louder still. The dragon's too big for this cave. I knew it upon first sight of him. We'll be crushed if we don't make it out before he awakens. The cave will be destroyed.

There's another crash, and Haime flinches. I slip from the ledge. This one was right behind me, and far too close for comfort.

"Go!" I shout again, and she finally disappears, taking the torch with her.

The light vanishes in moments. I pray that the way ahead of her is clear.

Pressing my foot to the wall, I use it as leverage and jump up. But my arms are still burning, they're shaking and won't take my weight. I slip back down. I do it again, harder this time, and miss again. Worried now, the heat building inside me, I try a third time and manage to fling one arm over to hold me up. A cacophony of noises blasts my ears as I climb my feet up the wall.

"Human!" a deep, guttural voice bellows. A deeply angered *male* voice. It fills the cave. It slams into my soul.

Stunned, I lose my footing and fall. My head slams into the ground. Searing pain darkens my mind.

Everything falls into the abyss.

I awake sometime later.

I don't know how long it's been. But time has passed because I'm surrounded by silence. Not even the shudder of pebbles reaches my ears. There's nothing but darkness and pain radiating from my head. For a while, all I can do is open and close my eyes, checking that my eyes really are opening because it's dark either way.

I lick my lips. *I need to move.*

I need...

Haime? Is she okay? I groan.

I manage to lift my arm and press my fingers to the back of my skull. My fingers come away sticky and I smell the blood. Tentatively, I return them to my head, trying to learn how badly I'm wounded. Wincing, I shut my eyes and discover a cut, nothing more. My hand drops and I smear what I can of my blood onto the ground, wiping the last of it on my top. When it's as clean as it'll get, I pull my legs into me and brace my elbow on the ground.

Pain like lightning shoots through my head, and I cry out. But I remember the dragon and I hush.

I wait, listening, wondering if he's still around, if he even heard me, but as nothing tackles me, I start to calm. The more I calm, the more tired I become. Part of me wants to curl up and sleep, hoping I'll wake up later, pain-free and back in my hut. If only life were that easy.

Move, Milaye. You can't stay here. You're not safe.

Clenching my teeth, I fight the exhaustion and rise into a sitting position. My head clouds. Luckily, I still have my supplies with me, and I tug forward the satchel strapped to my back. Digging through it, I feel for my bag of herbs and pull it out.

One by one, I sniff them until I find the one I'm looking for. Crushed Mermaid's Breath. A strong underwater flower the merfolk brings us that dulls pain. I gather saliva in my mouth and pinch some of the herb onto my tongue. I squinch, swallowing it.

It leaves a bad taste behind, but that's the least of my concerns.

By the time I put the herb away and strap my bag tight to my shoulder, my head and bruised body have already numbed out.

Now, it's time to move.

I slowly pull myself to my feet, keeping my arms forward to search the area directly around me. Dust and dirt fall off my skin.

I fell by the ledge. If I can find it again, maybe I'll discover my way out.

A groan reaches my ears, and I stiffen.

It's so quiet, had I actually heard something? I wait and am about to move forward when I hear it again. It's low and short and makes my chest constrict. My skin rises, and I take a step in the sound's direction before I realize what I'm doing.

It's him. Instinctively, I know it's him.

My dragon.

I picture his giant body, purple and black with scales like jewels, and my heart races. Beautiful, enchanting, and deadly.

He wasn't dead though.

A touch couldn't bring something back to life. As a huntress who has taken much life and seen my fair share of death, I know this.

But I *did* touch him and know what that means. Anxiety and excitement fill me. *I touched him.* Even if it had been by accident. *Haime touched him too.*

Though I know I'm the one who's bonded.

He's mine. He's alive, and he's mine. All that I've heard from Aida and Issa about their dragon bonds comes crashing back to me. That the dragon no longer exists, but a male does in its place. If I die, he dies, and if he dies, I die. That there is no way to sever the bond, and we're now mated for life, whether we want to be or not.

I could have a family. My body shakes. I could have the adoring gaze of a child looking up at me. *Me.* Because I would be its mother. I could be wanted, truly wanted, and not just another female of the tribe, a woman to be overlooked because she's only as good as what she can provide for others.

I'm almost stupefied into excitement, hope—and a fair amount of renewed worry—when another one of my dragon man's pained groans reaches my ears. My hand clutches my chest where the heat within builds.

I—I can't leave him behind.

I physically can't. The thought disturbs me. All I want to do is journey deeper into this dark, dangerous hole and find him, even if I die in the process. I take a step forward, now that I'm paying attention, I know exactly what direction he's in. *It must be the bond.*

Zaeyr and Aida are never more than thirty feet away from each other, and only when one of them is chasing after their children. They told me once that it's unnatural to be any farther apart, like a deep, uncomfortable coldness takes hold inside. And that pain has only worsened over the years.

Spanning my arms out, I partially crouch and make my way deeper, listening intently for more groans.

I come across rocks and boulders and stub my foot numerous times with pieces that have fallen. The ground is no longer level. I slide my feet forward carefully so as not to accidentally trip into a gap.

Another groan reaches my ears. My heart quickens, and I

struggle to keep my safe, slow pace. An aroma fills my nostrils, heady and wild. Like what a midnight storm might smell like, if it had a smell. I breathe it in and nearly moan from delight.

His scent is intoxicating.

The warmth in my chest descends to my sex. I clench. It does so with every inhale. My mind muddles. I shouldn't want to mate right now... but I desperately do. I press my hands to my pelvis, eager to reach under my skirt and seek relief—but I stop myself.

What's wrong with me? I breathe in the male's midnight storm again, unable to do otherwise. I grow wet, and my arousal slickens my thighs. In moments, I'm dripping and ready.

He could be grotesque—a monster—and I'd still want to mate him, just from the way he smells. As if his male spice was created for me and me alone.

And as if he knows what's happening to me, he groans again, and this time it's long and winded. *His breaths have quickened like my heart.* I listen to him as I drop to my knees and crawl forward.

My hands find him, and I stop.

His groans have stopped too.

7

———

DRAZAK SUCCUMBS

PAIN RIPS through me as I lie in the dark, still unable to move. Recalling the human's touch is the only thing that brings my mind respite.

Because I moved. Her touch changed me but it also powered over the strength of the poison.

I lost my majestic body, but for a short time, I moved. I *felt* again. Any misgivings that I had about dying paralyzed in an unknown body are gone. I will gratefully be human if I could move freely again.

My wings shifted, my legs stretched out, and for a glorious second, I thought I might rise from this dark prison and ascend into the sky. Retake my territory. Reclaim my land and reek terror on all within.

I tasted blissful freedom.

Instead of breaking through the ground, roaring to the heavens in triumph, my body convulsed in on itself, my wings folded into my skin, and my teeth fell from my mouth. Pain came next, unlike I have ever known, breaking my mind, and through it all, I could hear the human... *Humans*, I correct, through it all. There were two. And though one smelled entic-ing, the other was strangely scented of my kind.

They ran from my torment after causing it, leaving me to my fate.

They had run, but first, one of them bonded with me. I hope it is the one whose smell I'd dared enjoy.

Luckily, the cave fell apart without killing me. If I could move once, I can do so again. *Perhaps the venom will not affect me as a human the same way it had as a dragon.*

Once the pain of my transformation is gone, I *will* my new limbs to tense. And for a moment, they do. I continue, even when my new body tires.

Eventually, the last of the rocks fall, and the cave grows quiet as I work my muscles. I do not know how much time has passed since my change, but I know I am no longer as strong as I used to be. I stop straining and listen to the last bits of dust and dirt drop from above. Some of it lands on my new, naked flesh.

I am cold, I realize. I have never felt cold before.

But I am hot as well. Inside—where my fire used to blaze— is an inferno. The heat does not rest in one spot like it used to, but rushes through my veins to every corner of my new human body. Worst yet, it pools into my shaft and...to my sudden excitement, hardens it.

My mind temporarily blanks. I am overcome with lust.
Lust!

A dragon's lust is feverish—or so I have heard—and hard to master. It comes on hot and quick when a femdragon's heated pheromones bloom on the air, and all dragonkind who smell it succumb to its effects.

But I am a dragon no more. Yet, the ache in my shaft threatens to steal my mind and take control of me. I try to grasp it, but once again, all I can do is strain my muscles and twitch my puny human toes.

Skies!

My mind reels. *My body seeks to mate when it cannot even move! Just like how I feared it would!* Anger and shame mixes with keen desire. The *desire* to have something hot, tight, and willing to take my shaft, to alleviate it for me.

Move, dark skies. Move, you petrified weak body! My nostrils flare. A throaty groan rumbles from me.

I smell a familiar scent.

Sweat and sea salt, jungle lilies and spice. My thoughts turn to it though my prick jerks. *I know this smell. It is the human's scent. Was it the one who touched me?*

My... *lips?*... ease open, and I groan again. Inhaling—my chest rises and falls with the effort. It is stronger and clearer this time. She is to my right—I know because I sense her. She is the human who touched me, who bonded me to her.

She did not leave me.

She is nearing. The reason I am in this predicament. A fresh burst of excitement assaults me. I hear her now, her slow, shuffling movements in the dark, coming ever nearer.

I would forgive her touch, if only I could move.

She is close. Are human senses this keen? Or is it the bond? If I were facing her way, I would be able to see her in the dark. Instead, all I can see is the shadowy grooves of the broken and tree-root clogged ceiling above. I have not lost all my dragon's gifts.

I hope.

I know much about humans, as I do all enemies of my kind, but it has been a long time, and I never sought to gain knowledge from those of my dragon kin who have bonded to humans.

Anticipation builds as the shuffling noises stop.

But the more I think about it, the more I wonder if this human is only here because she is trapped here, like I am. *Is she here for me or because she has no other choice?*

Why do I care?

Her scent thickens, and I am overwhelmed. Gone are the flowers and sweat. They have been replaced by sweet, mesmerizing ambrosia. The inferno in my body explodes, sizzling every fiber. I want to bathe in it, bask in her sweet scent, find the spot where it is coming from and bury my snout... *nose?*... into it. My mouth waters to bring that smell to my tongue so I may taste and drink it down.

She is in heat. She must be. My shaft grows harder. All I want to do is squeeze and pump it in my hand.

If I did not think I was cursed before...

There is movement beside me. Something touches my skin. I quiet my groaning as my need detonates. The female gasps, and her warm touch stills. It is her fingers, I realize, up against my side. They are on me. The female is touching me. Awe clouds my mind.

"Are...are you okay?" she asks hesitantly and—and I understand her! Her words make sense. *I spoke her language in fury when I transformed. Human.* The entirety of her words and meaning are clear to me.

I try to answer, but my lips do not move. My tongue remains stiff.

I try to speak again. Nothing. My frustration builds. I wait for her to do something more, to please my ears with the sound of her voice, but she does not.

She waits for my response.

Skies!

I am at her mercy, at the mercy of everything in this world. She could easily leave, or kill me—anything could happen at this point. I need her to survive. I have never needed another being after my mother and sire reared me. Part of me wants to lash out, to bellow at this sudden weakness.

Worse yet, her hands have not moved. The spots where they lie are now burning me with the contact. I want them to move, need them to move. It is agony, not being able to take what I want, to force her into action. I moan as compellment.

"Dragon man?" she says with frustrating hesitancy.

Dragon man? I scoff. *So she knows of the dragon's bane.* She knows what she has turned me into. A small bit of anger needles me. But her voice is melodious and strong, and takes away my anger.

If this female can brave the wilds and survive, she must be strong. Why do I care what she calls me?

Her hands shift on my skin, and all other cares vanish. They move from my side to slide onto my belly, warm and curious. They do not linger but move up and over my chest, testing every inch of my exposed flesh. They press lightly into me as if they are exploring something new... or checking for wounds. As they move, I try to strain my muscles beneath them, testing them for the same reasons.

There is no pain. Not anymore. Not except for my throbbing shaft.

And like warm, soothing feathers, the female's fingers continue up and down my arms, doing the same as they did with my chest. I learn my new form from her and find that I am fit and built. I also discover that not all of my scales are gone, as there are places her warmth fades and my body is rigid and not surrendering to her prodding.

My mind reels from sensation. The last creature to touch me did so in hopes to kill me. This is different, unexpected.

Even enjoyable.

The female's hands are soft, yet wary, like she does not want to hurt me. They end up on my face, where they explore my features. Her fingers trace my jaw, my lips—which causes my shaft to twitch—and up my human nose. They whisper across my cheeks to trace around my eyes, but stop when they reach my brow.

My dark jewel.

I still have it?

Pride and relief infuse me. Dark dragons, since they are not born of natural elements, create a central piece to draw strength from. My jewel formed when I was a young dragonling, starving for darkness to nourish me.

The female examines it, making me shiver. Pleasure stokes my lust and my need to mate grows.

Then I see her.

Her form is blurred in the impermeable darkness my body has created. I can only make out some of her features, and my eyes trail across them as curiously as her hands on me.

She is dirty. There are smudges of dust from the cave-in all over her skin. I inhale again, searching for the scent of blood through the heady aroma of her natural scent, and find it. I do not like that I smell it, finding I am worried for her—and that perturbs me further. I should not care whether she is hurt or not, but I do.

My fingers shake. I care. A lot.

She is moving. She cannot be hurt that badly. The thought does not give me comfort.

I search her face and what I can see of her body, but I do not see the wound. Wherever it is, it is hidden from me. My eyes retreat to her face, and this time, I take the time to study it.

I have never been this close to a human before. In my prime, I saw them from afar, peering down at them from the skies. They ran and screamed as I burned down their villages. Despite my mischief, I have never been close enough to discern the delicacies of their features.

Though the darkness stole the human's coloring, I can tell she has dark eyes and dark hair, which is long, straight, and pulled away from her face to hang in a messy cinch over her shoulder. Long enough that if it were not tied back, it would be flooding over me, tickling my skin. There are things in her hair as well—feathers perhaps? Or shells? I cannot be certain at my angle.

She is wearing coverings over her chest. Leather, I assume. Animal hide? But perhaps sewn grass. It reminds me how frail humans are and that I lack my own coverings.

There are bands on her arms and wrists, and what I suspect are weapons attached to her body. Beneath them, her body appears smooth and healthy.

Except for the blood I smell.

Her eyes stare aimlessly into the dark, and I enjoy the fact that she cannot see me studying her. But many of her features remain distorted despite my ability.

I discover something odd... I wish to see more.

I am forever bonded to this creature, I remind myself. Any intelligent being would be curious to know more, to learn who they are chained to.

The female's fingers leave my jewel and discover my horns. *Horns!* I am also thrilled to have retained these. *Horns that I will use to protect us.*

My desire to take her and mate catapults inside me. Blood rushes to my loins, becoming excruciating.

I hear her gasp, and it burns. Her hands pull away from me, and I miss their touch immediately.

What I would do if I could move... Take her hands and place them back on me. No... I would do more than that. I would pull her into my arms, bury my nose to her neck, and cover her body with mine.

I practically pant at the thought.

Her breathing labors to match my thundering heart, and I know she is as affected by the bond as I am. I can *feel* her want for me echo back.

Thankfully, her hands return to my body to probe at my chest. Pleasure jolts me, but her fingers do not remain there long. They are moving down, down, down... They reach my pelvis, and I hold my breath. My shaft rests hard and ready on my thigh. Her fingers slow but stay away from my root, frustrating me. They brush against it—stars fill my vision—but they jerk away and move down my thighs.

And then they are gone, down my legs, searching for wounds I know are not there. Torture and bliss all at once. I vow to make her feel the same once I am free of this poisonous trap... A growl escapes my lips, though it comes out as another groan.

Her perusal ends at my feet, but then grows strangely wild when she finds one of my tails. She finds the other one soon after.

They are limp in her hand.

She finally lifts her hands from me, and this time, does not return them, but at least she moves back up that I may view her again. She gazes into the void, unseeing. She brings her hands to her lips, where she cups them together.

I wait for her next move, curious what she will do.

"I'm going to try and find something to start a fire with," she whispers. Her hands drop to her sides. "Don't... don't move. I'll be back soon."

Fire? Unease niggles me. I should be the one to take care of my mate. That is the dragon's way. Not this.

But she is already gone, removed from my sight.

I want to tell her not to go, that I will not be down long, but the words do not come out.

And I am left with the unsettling scent of her blood in my nostrils and the quiet noises she makes as she moves through my cave... farther and farther away from me.

8

———

TRAPPED

It DOESN'T TAKE me long to find what I need for a fire. Luckily, I discovered broken roots that had fallen with the cave's roof. I don't expect they'll burn well, but I'm excited to have light again soon.

Because I need to see the dragon male. There's an image in my mind of a fiend, and it frightens me. A creature with multiple tails and horns. I don't know what to make of his forehead. I know he's a human male, but my imagination runs wild...

Gathering a cluster of roots, I pick one out to light and set the remainder aside. I pull off my satchel and search for my fire moss and flint. After rubbing the fire moss on the end of the root, I take out my dagger and cut off a little bit of my hair for kindling. It takes several tries, but I manage to start a small flame. Wrinkling my nose, I grab the root and stick it into my kindling. It blazes to life.

Golden light casts around me. *I can see again!* I could cry for such a small miracle.

Blinking several times, my eyes adjust, and I hold up my

makeshift torch and peer around me. All I see is rocks, debris, and darkness.

Not wanting to waste time, I gather my things and look for the dragon man again.

When I hear a raspy moan. I head in that direction. *Thank the waters I don't have to stumble about in search of him...*

He's hurt. He has to be. Why else hasn't he risen? I didn't find a wound, but that doesn't mean there wasn't one. It reminds me of my wound. My fingers twitch to check on it. *I'll need another dose of Mermaid's Breath soon.* I'm weakening.

The dragon male's body comes into view. He sparkles where my light reaches him, purple and glassy black. Brilliant and breathtaking. My eyes widen. My jaw drops. If I didn't already know he was once the giant dragon, I would now. His scales are unmistakable.

I move to him and drop to my knees. A blush rises to my cheeks. My head clouds when I scent him.

He's... I swallow. *He's beautiful.*

Dark and—I lick my lips as my eyes trail over his body—*unlike anything in Venys.*

I see his hard prick and quickly glance away. *And naked. He's naked and primed.* I suck in my stomach. I *will* my lust away, but it builds instead. Closing my eyes hard, I force myself to remember the situation we're in. That we're both hurt. That we don't even know each other. It doesn't work—I'm still lustful—but I reopen my eyes and manage to focus on creating a fire anyway.

I don't know how hurt he is. I can't waste time.

Piling the roots I gathered, I sprinkle fire moss over them and ignite them. The cave opens to my view as the flames roar upward. Soothing heat blankets my skin, and I sigh in satisfaction.

"I hope this helps," I say, turning to the male. I don't know if he's awake enough to hear me or if he even understands, but I say it anyway. Pulling off my satchel, I shuffle to his side. Now with more light, I can see him clearly.

He's got two sets of horns, that's for sure, and a jewel embedded on his brow. Frowning, I notice wisps of black smoke rising from it, like it had when he was still in his true form. I recall the glassy feel from when I'd searched him for injuries, but I don't know what the jewel is to him or why it is there. I want to touch it again but decide not to. *It may hurt him, or me.*

He's got unkempt ebony hair that's long enough to pool on the ground around his head. I dare to brush my fingers over him and move several strands from his face. My fingers flutter over his horns—there are four—but drop soon after.

My eyes dip.

Lo and behold, he does have two tails. They're lax at his side next to my knees, but they're under him and lifting his hips off the floor. *That can't be comfortable.* But there's nothing I can do about it right now. I won't move him until I know what's wrong with him.

Setting my torch on the far side of him, I sit back and straighten.

"I can see now," I tell him. "I'm going to touch you again to see what's wrong."

I check his face for a response, but there isn't one, not even a groan. His eyes are closed, but I could have sworn they were open earlier, when my fingers traced his face. I shake my head.

"I'll try not to hurt you," I add.

Carefully, I shift my hands under his head, sliding my fingers through his hair. It's silken and so fine that I'm temporarily distracted by the feel of it. I suck in my stomach and force myself to move on.

Pressing into his skull, I feel for a wound like mine but find none. I remove my hands.

I was certain he hit his head. It had to be his head, right? If he's unconscious?

He's warm to the touch, and his chest rises and falls, so I know he's alive, just not responding.

"Dragon?" I ask hesitantly.

Again, he doesn't respond.

He's unconscious. Has to be. Which doesn't bode well for us if he remains this way for long. There's nothing wanting to eat us right now, but that doesn't mean it'll stay that way. I look around.

We'll have to spend the night here... Assuming it's night. I turn back around, facing where I believe the ledge once was. *I need to see if the opening still exists.*

I can't put it off forever.

Turning back to the dragon, I reach over and take hold of my torch. "I need to leave again, scout for a way out and make sure we're safe. I'll be back soon." I don't want to leave him, but I rise anyway.

He groans.

I frown. *So he is awake? Is he faking?* Something tells me he's not...

"I promise I'll be right back," I whisper. "I won't leave you. I won't be going far."

When I step away, no groan stops me.

Brandishing my torch, I head into the cavern and make my way toward the nearest wall. It's different than before—which I already knew—with dust and dirt everywhere. When I come across the larger boulders, I'm thankful none of them hit Haime or me... or the male now in my care.

What am I going to do about him?

We can't stay here. I don't have the strength to move him. It's dangerous beyond measure, staying here. The naga boy is gone, but where did he go and who was he with? Besides, I hate being confined in enclosed spaces. If I need to run, I don't like worrying about not having an exit.

I can't leave him. Not while he's so defenseless. He's a male, a humanoid male now, which makes him extremely precious—incredibly rare. And not only that, he's mine now. We're linked. Even now, the bond between us is growing stronger, and I sense... My brow creases. I sense a heaviness inside me. It wants me to stop moving. My muscles are stiff when my mind lingers on it.

There's something inside him that shouldn't be there.

I don't know how I know it, but I do. I clench my fingers then loosen them, fighting off the stiffness.

I need to find Haime, I realize with an uncomfortable jolt. *Need to know if she needs me, if she's safe.* A fresh wave of tiredness washes me and a niggling of fear threatens to worm its way in. *She's safe.* I have to believe it. *She made it out, and the way is clear...*

She's probably already back at the tribe, and help is on the way.

I come to the wall, and this time it doesn't take me long to find the ledge. Placing my torch on top of it, I grip it and jump, using my momentum to haul myself up. Stars shoot over my vision as I drop onto my back and rest for a moment. I press my hand to the back of my head and wince.

The next second, I'm back on my feet and searching for the entrance. I find it quickly. Thank the waters. Ducking into the crevasse, I make my way down the path.

I reach the fork and find my shells still on the ground. There's some dirt on them but I leave them for later. Turning toward the exit, I move slowly, knowing the walls will close in. Tree roots gnarl around me.

Then it occurs to me... Why Haime hasn't come back to check on me? Has she waited or gone to the tribe like I hoped? Fear takes hold.

The dirt loosens under my sandals, and the walls narrow

even more. I stop, staring at them. The pathway's gone, vanished under rocks and roots. My mind blanks, my heart races. I take a deep breath to stop my rising panic.

Lowering my torch, I press both hands against the obstruction and gently push. Nothing gives but for some loose dirt that crumbles to the ground. I press again, same result.

My nails bite into the dirt.

Don't panic, Milaye. Don't. But my throat tightens anyway. *Haime's made it to the other side, I know she has. She's a stubborn little dragon girl, she wouldn't let some cave-in beat her.*

"Okay, there has to be another way out," I tell myself. "There's another path." Taking one last look at the blocked path, I wipe the dirt off my hands, grab my torch, and turn back. At the fork, I step over my shells and make my way down the other path. Only a few steps in and it's already curving sharply to the right. I follow it for a time, not realizing how far and deep it goes. It is also getting smaller and tighter. I grow uneasy and keep my free palm on the hilt of my dagger.

Each step shoots a chill through my veins.

I'm getting farther from *him*.

When it occurs to me that there's no end in sight, I pause. My vision is beginning to blur.

But I take another step anyway.

Leaning against the cave wall to rest, I place my hand to my heart and feel it thunder under my palm. I roll my head to the side, pressing my brow upon the stone wall. Its coolness gives me a moment of ease, and I check the wound on the back of my head, squeezing my eyes shut when there's pain.

What am I going to do?

Tears threaten to fall, and I almost release them... *I'm not trapped. We're not trapped.* There's a way out of this. I'm sure of it. There's no time for tears, not right now. Just because the entrance is shut and this path spirals downward, it doesn't mean all is lost. I have to hope. *I'll do everything I can to survive.*

If I wallow now, I'm not Milaye, Protector of the Mermaid Coast, leader of Sand's Hunters Huntresses, and Watcher of the Young. I'll dig my way out if I have to.

I right myself.

But it pains me to imagine taking another step forward, knowing the bond will protest. *I'll have to come back later when I'm stronger... when he's stronger. I've lost a lot of blood.*

And I'm getting so tired. It's unsafe for me to wander around in the dark, risking my life when there's someone who needs me.

The male's face surfaces in my mind. A rush of warmth floods me, and for a moment, I'm revitalized. My panicked heart calms, and a small smile lifts my lips. It gives me enough strength to keep pushing through my exhaustion, my fear.

If I can stumble upon a rare dragon and he can become a man, then anything is possible, right? Even surviving this.

I make up my mind.

We'll escape together.

I turn around and go back to him.

9

DRAZAK AND THE INVADER

I HATE that she can leave me at any moment and I am powerless to stop her. All I have to remind me she was here at all is her delicious, lingering scent and the fire beside me. Its crackles fill my ears, making it harder to hear my human as she gets farther and farther away.

Then there is the smoke the fire gives off. It is bitter and strong, and to my frustration, the longer it burns, the more it clears away the human's smell. Soon, it will be gone, and I will be alone again.

A growl tears from my throat. I open my eyes and gaze in the direction she went.

Human, come back. Another growl comes forth. *First, you bind yourself to me, and now you leave willingly?* The daring of this female frustrates me.

I do not even know what she looks like. I kept my eyes closed when she lit the fire. The sudden light hurt too much for me to bear. But I am healing, I realize, and with each minute that passes, the poison dragon's toxin lessens within me. Liquid beads my usually cold body—from the fire, no less—and it is helping me expel the poison's effects.

Perhaps that was all I needed these long years—a way to sweat it out of me. If dragons could sweat...

Why has she not returned? My weak human fingers twitch at my sides. *She should be here where I can see her. Can protect...*

Yet another growl expels from me. I cannot protect anything, not even myself right now.

A dragon male protects his mate. That is his sole duty after his mate has been claimed and seeded. Until a dragonling is born, and even then, the male remains, lingering until the dragonling is grown enough to protect itself—then and only then do the femdragon and offspring leave.

But dragons bond differently with humans. That bond is unique because of the red comet that shifted Venys. When the comet first appeared, the world twisted, and all species upon it suffered.

The red comet brings out the heat in dragons—the wild urge to reproduce. It was a boon as much as it was a curse.

I do not know whatever blight fell upon the other species of Venys from the comet. It had never been my concern.

I have missed many comets though, I am certain... stuck in this cave. Does Venys even suffer the red comet anymore? For all I know it is possible, after all, long ago when I was young, the red comet did not exist.

Is this why a female human has found me? Is the red comet in the sky at this very moment? My tails lift and my fingers curl. Bond or not, my need to mate is powerful. And with a human female no less. *Where is she!?*

As soon as I can rise...

Thoughts whirl through my head. *She will never leave my side again, and I—I will reclaim all that has been taken from me! I will start with her.*

I flick my tails, purposely this time. And that... that is everything. Excitement joins my annoyance. I may never fly, but I will be able to eat and rut. I will be able to run and hunt. I will be able to move again.

I can search for the bones of the poison dragon and ruin them.

But first... *Where is my human?* My nostrils flare. Too much time has passed.

My human is hurt, I know this. Is the hurt on her head? I like it less and less that I cannot rise to care for her. My gaze shifts to the cave ceiling, and I watch the golden cast of the fire's light dance over it. It is an easy trance, and it dulls the pain I sense from her. I can be stable while she is in the dark.

A hissing noise pricks my ears. A second later, it happens again, louder this time.

My eyes drift from the fire, searching for the source.

I see something move. A long and angular mass. It slowly gets bigger. It pauses when I move, managing to drop my head to the side. The first thing I notice is its tail-like body, it's gaunt frame.

Not a human. I inhale. *It is not the other human who was with mine from earlier.* But I know this already...because of the tail.

A naga?

White and yellow eyes pierce the shadows to pin mine.

This time when I growl, a growl comes out. The naga does not flee, but it also does not come closer. I strain and flex again, urging my body to do something, anything. If the naga attacks, there will be nothing I can do to defend myself. Nagas are base beasts of the jungle, a staple of any dragon's diet.

I taste its flesh in my memories.

The beady yellow dots of its eyes flash in the dark. I am prime food offered up on a platter. Any beast as gaunt as this one would not balk at the opportunity to engorge.

I manage to make a fist with my hand closest to it, bracing, readying it. I do not want to die, and I growl again, but the noise is not nearly as loud or as frightening as it used to be.

I wait for the attack but the naga only stares at me.

What is he waiting for?

Suddenly, the bond inside me flares up. I hear my human's footsteps. *No!* My useless body goes rigid.

"*Watch out,*" I try to say in my human's language, but it comes out as a gurgle. I try to move my head in her direction, but I fail.

The naga hisses once more, a warning, and then slithers back into the darkness.

"You're awake," my human gasps, dropping next to me with a huff. Her hands cup my face and shift my head so I might face her. My eyes linger, staying on the spot the naga disappeared.

When her face fills my vision, I am struck by her beauty. "*Naga,*" I warn. "*Not safe.*" It comes out a croak.

Her brows furrow. "Grala no safee?"

"*Naga.*"

She shakes her head.

I flick my eyes back to the shadows.

And she gets it, glancing up. Her lips flatten, and she pulls out a sharp weapon from her side. Pride swells. *My human is brave.*

She stands with her fire stick and steps over me. I lose sight of her. Fear for her safety gives me the strength to thrash my tails and lift one hand—but it thumps to the ground.

If she is hurt on my account, I will perish dishonorably. I will never forgive myself!

I claw the dirt.

I can do nothing but wait, nervous that any sound might be the last sound I ever do from her. *I had only gotten a glimpse of my human. A single look.* It is not enough and never will be.

Then her footsteps reappear, and relief temporarily strangles me. Her leg falls into my vision as she steps back over me and sits down to face me.

Her eyes meet mine. Dark brown orbs framed in thick black

lashes with striking, arched brows.

I capture them to memory. *We have only just met, and yet I am uncertain if we will live long enough to know each other.*

Her eyes flicker away and peer around us, and my human cants her head. *She is listening for something. For the naga I saw.* Knowing it is still there bothers me greatly. I hope that it will not return until I can rise. My fingers continue to curl at my sides.

"I didn't find anything," she says. "But I laid out some shells and some sticks in case there is something."

I do not understand, but she places her dagger at her side instead of putting it away. That is enough to assure me she is being vigilant.

She glances out again into the dark, and her eyes vacant as if she is lost in thought.

"I won't leave you again unless I absolutely have to." She looks back at me. "The cave..." She shakes her head. "We're in a cavern of some sort, and there's a path that leads out." Her lips purse. I am momentarily distracted by how full and enticing they are. "There's a path, but it goes too deep, and I was getting too far away... When you're better, we'll leave together." Concern etches her face, at least what I think is concern.

She is not telling me something. Has she discovered something I do not know?

She is concerned for me.

I part my lips. "Not safe," I say. I am concerned for her too.

"Not safe?" she asks.

Yes! I groan in agreement.

Her head drops. "You can understand me," her voice lowers. "I'll protect us until you're well. It seems this cave is deserted."

Deserted? Frustration spikes.

"Why can't you move?" she asks. "Did I... cause this when I fell on you?"

Fell on me? I hmph. No human would pass up the opportunity to steal a dragon. But then I remember her presence, how she'd explored me before I transformed, how she did not bind me at the first opportunity.

The naga did not attack me either.

Has Venys changed so much? Have the creatures gone mad?

Her gaze steadies on me. *She is waiting for me to answer. What should I tell her?* I do not want to share my shame. That I was struck by a lesser dragon, that I was brought down? That I allowed a human to touch me without putting up a fight...

For some reason I am not as bothered by that, not as I should be... not as I was before it happened. I am waiting for her to touch me again, I realize. *And if she falls this time, I will catch her.*

If I could just get up!

"Poison," I answer.

She stares at me before nodding. "What bit you? Do you know? Or where?" She scans my body.

I tense, wanting her to like what she sees.

Am I pleasing? I know horns and tails are not human traits, nor are scales and claws—my dark jewel—but could she overlook them?

If she recoils from me...

She bites down on her lip and turns away. My chest constricts. *She finds me repugnant.* I close my eyes in embarrassment.

Something thuds, and I hear a rip of cloth. I reopen my eyes to discover what she is doing and find the scraps of her bag hanging in her hands. She drops it over my jutting shaft with a squeak and threads it under my hips. Confused, I try to lift them to help her. Her warm skin is on me again and my embarrassment fades long enough to enjoy the pleasure of having her near. Then her hands find the base of my tails.

I moan.

She stops what she is doing but her hands and the bunched

cloth remains.

"I'm sorry," she says quickly, shaking her head. Her cheeks have gone red.

I do not respond. Her hands move to tie the cloth into place. I peer down.

She has covered my root, I realize. And not in the way I would have preferred.

She shifts, and our eyes meet. "I should have covered you sooner," she says.

I part my mouth to argue—

"I'll look for that bite now," she mutters, beginning to circle back down me, wandering out of my line of sight.

"No bite." I stop her. "Wounds healed long ago." My voice is clipped.

"No bite?"

"No."

She returns. Her dark eyes capture mine again. *Skies, is she lovely. I may not be to her liking but she is to mine.*

"Is it something you ate?" she asks.

"No."

"Something that touched you, something you absorbed?"

"No."

She sits back. "How can I help you then? What can I do?"

Stay here with me. Do not leave my side. Make sure I can see you at all times so I do not worry. But I do not tell her this. "Rest," I respond. Though this is not what I need, it is what she *needs*.

Knowing there is a naga lurking somewhere in the dark unnerves me. *She needs to rest, to regain her strength, and I... I need to get the skies up!*

"Rest... Okay, rest it is." She nods.

She goes quiet as we stare at each other. Her mouth opens and closes several times as if she has more she wants to say, but she remains silent. Her hand lifts to the back of her head, and she winces. It comes away with blood.

Her wound. My face tightens.

"Rest," I order.

She straightens and drops her hand. "No. I'll keep watch."

I will not have it. My eyes narrow. "You rest. I do not... need it..."

"And if something attacks?" Exhaustion etches her face. She cannot hide it from me. She needs sleep more than I.

"I will... wake you. Rest," I order again. I will not have my orders disobeyed, not by a human. Not by *my* human. "I have... good hearing. I will wake you."

She sucks her lower lip into her mouth but nods. "All right, I will rest."

Another wave of pleasure floods me. *She knows to trust me. This, I can do for her.*

She lies down beside me, just shy of touching me. I shift my hand, managing to press it to her arm. She does not remove it. I drop my head to the side. She is gazing back at me, her eyelids half-closed.

"Drazak," I tell her. "My name is Drazak."

She will fall asleep with my name in her mind.

She smiles softly, and my heart seizes.

"Drazak," she breathes, saying my name back to me. "I'm Milaye."

"Milaye." I like it. It is sweet on the tongue. "Sleep now, Milaye. I will listen."

Her eyes close, but her smile remains. And as her breathing softens, I take her in, wondering how much my life has changed in such a short amount of time. I lose myself in her nearness. Her sun-kissed skin. Her inviting lips. The way the firelight flickers across her face. It gives me the strength to keep working at my body.

Her lips become my goal.

And I listen and listen intently, knowing despite this quiet moment, we are surrounded by danger.

74

10

____

RECEDING DARKNESS

SOMETHING TUGS AT MY HAIR, pinching it away from my skin, and I moan. Ticklish prickles shoot from my scalp, through my body. I long to bask in it, but the haze of sleep clears from my head. The pain returns.

Gone is the pleasure, and I groan, batting my hand at whatever's in my hair. _If Haime thinks waking me is... That's not Haime's hand._ My eyes shoot open. There's a strange and wicked male in front of me.

A male! In my cot?

My lips part to scream but then recognition hits. _Drazak._

The cave. The dragon.

His eyes catch mine as he traps my hand, clenching my fingers between his. Heat surges, and my sex clenches. My legs twitch. I try not to show how much his touch does to me. How much I want him. How inappropriate the timing is for all of this.

Don't glance at his groin. Don't.

It's so hard not to. I have a feeling his shaft is as hard as ever. And with mortification, I hope I'm right.

"I did not mean to... wake you." His voice is rich and deep, no longer raspy. His words are clearer. His voice coils around me.

"How long have I been asleep?" My fingers flex against his, and his hold on my hand tightens.

"A while."

He brings our hands between us, resting them on the ground. His engulfs mine, and even in the flickering shadows between our bodies, I'm dazzled by the purple twinkle of his scales. Even as my eyes lock on his short black claws.

"I'm glad you woke me." I swallow thinking what those claws could do to me. I itch to stroke them and see if they're as sharp as they appear. My gaze flicks back to meet his when he squeezes my hand.

"I am not. You are weak. I should have kept my hand to myself."

"I'm not weak." Indignation wipes away any lingering traces of sleep. I rise.

"Stay," he pleads, keeping my hand hostage. "I do not mean it as an insult... I smell your blood."

After a moment, I drop back down. At being mentioned, my head throbs and I wince. "You can smell it?"

"Yes."

"It's just a gash," I reassure him because there's concern on his face. "It's nothing to worry about."

"I caused it," he rumbles.

"I fell. I lost my grip."

"When running for safety when I transformed." There's accusation in his voice.

True, but I don't tell him that. The way he's gazing at me, the way his brow furrows, it makes me think he's profoundly unhappy about my wound. I don't know how to take it. "I'll be fine. And you're—" my eyes widen "—you're moving." I sit up and check out his body.

He's shifted. Now he is on his side with his arms reaching

before him, the one that had taken my hand now placed palm down on the ground, holding his weight. And he *is* holding himself up, slightly, using his arm as a prop. His tails are behind him, and his other arm lies under his cheek.

I realize he's been watching me. It would be easy to do so in this position. That he may have been watching for some time.

His eyes twinkle. "I am making progress."

I scrape my teeth across my bottom lip.

"Your voice is clearer now too," I say.

"It has not been used in many years. It is strange to speak again."

I remember his unmoving dragon form. "How long?" I pull my legs under me and rummage through my scattered belongings for my rations of dried meat.

His dark eyes follow me. I know they do.

I can feel them like burning stabs.

"A long time," he says.

"You were... When I found you, I thought you were dead."

"I was sure I would die that way. Perhaps another hundred years or so, and I would have."

A hundred years or so...

He continues, "But you came."

I unwrap my dried meat and move back to Drazak's side. "Hundreds of years is a long time. That isn't close to being dead..."

"For a dragon it is."

I shake my head. "So you've... been down here a long time?" I can't even imagine it. "Hundreds of years?"

"Thousands, I believe."

My lips part. My eyes go wide. "How? How is that possible?"

"Dragons are immortal unless something comes along and kills us. We will not die otherwise. But I have been starving, unmoving for so long... I was weakening."

"From poison?"

His dark eyes glint again. "Yes."

We stare at each other. I wait for him to tell me more. He doesn't.

What could poison a dragon? If I struggle to wrap my head around his age, how could I understand the creature that could poison him? Drazak's dragon was gigantic. Hundreds of me put together would've still been smaller than his body's size. I've seen sea serpents off the coast and giant mountain eagles fly overhead, but nothing as large as he was.

What could possibly poison a massive creature like him?

I'm afraid to ask. Do I even want to know? Is having an answer worth the nightmares?

I hand him one of my rations. "I don't want you to starve," I whisper, changing the subject.

He looks at my offering.

"Wait!"

I set the meat aside and wrap my arms around him. He stiffens in my embrace.

He growls. "Let me do this. I will sit up on my own."

"You can sit up all you want later." I'm used to dealing with kids. "For now, I will help you while you heal."

Positioning myself behind him, I haul him into a sitting position, but when I start to let go, he drops. Indignant growls and curses fill my ears but I ignore them. Looking around I find a boulder a few feet behind him. Getting a better grip, I brace and drag him to the rock.

A few minutes—and lots of grunting—later, he's propped up against it.

Catching my breath and ignoring the renewed pressure in my head, I drop beside him and wipe the sweat off my brow. I'm strong, but he's still large for a human and much bigger than I am. *And he's got those tails, and those horns,* I moan. Horns I want to explore thoroughly.

Maybe even lick.

When I catch his eye, he's angry.

"I will not get any stronger if I am not given the opportunity to challenge myself," he snaps.

"You will not get better *at all* if you starve to death." I grab the rations. "Dragons may not have to eat for long periods, but humans must eat every day. You're human now. Mostly." I put the dried meat in his hand. His fingers wrap around it.

"Thanks to you," he grumbles.

There's a surge of guilt. "I—"

"I am moving again, *thanks to you.* I have not yet decided if that is a good thing. Though I never thought I would be bonded, lose my immortality, or my power, now I am able to perish with a voice again."

I can't tell if he's mad at me or not. "I am sorry, regardless."

"You know of the dragon's curse," he states it more than asks.

"Yes."

"Then why did you not claim me when you first came upon me?"

"First came—" my eyes flick to the jewel on his brow, and I watch the puffs of dark smoke coming from it "—upon you?"

"I heard you, felt the warmth of your fire stick. You were by my hindleg, then you were before me. Why did you not claim me?"

"It didn't feel right."

"Any human would bind a dragon if given half the chance. The bond does more than mate us for life, it also strips away our threat."

"I thought you were dead," I murmur.

His brows arch. "And you did not want to make sure?"

I shake my head, then wince. I rub the sore, swollen flesh at the back of my head. Drazak's eyes narrow, and I see through the corner of my vision his hands shake and clench.

"You were beautiful," I tell him, ignoring his reaction. "I've...

searched for you for so long that I'd given up. I no longer had hope that I'd see a dragon one day, let alone bond with one... You were beautiful, and I—I didn't want to change that. I couldn't, not like that. Not so my hopes could come true. It felt wrong. It felt selfish."

"A mistake, human."

"Mistake?"

"For not taking the opportunity when it presented itself."

"And you would have? If the roles were reversed?"

He glances at the meat in his hand. "Do you want to be bound to me?"

Taken aback, I stare at him. It's a question I don't know how to answer. *Yes*, I want to scream, but then the part of me that approaches with caution—with every possible outcome already played out in her head—hesitates. "I'd given up," I repeat, as if that's an answer.

His jaw ticks. "Why?"

"Because only the lucky among my tribe are given the honor to mate."

"And you did not have that honor?"

His questions make me uncomfortable. No one else ever cared enough to ask these questions, and I don't know what to do about it. As a protector of Sand's Hunters, all my tribe cares about is that I perform my duties and that I remain healthy enough to continue doing so.

Perhaps that's why I love our children so much. I gaze down at my hands, feeling my chest squeeze. The tribe's children are so sweet and innocent and loving. You never had to wonder if you were loved by them. You knew it the moment they wrapped their little arms around you with laughter.

"No. I did not have that honor," I say.

Drazak lifts his free hand, and I look up to see what he's doing. Slowly, he brings it to my face and rubs the back of his finger up my cheek. Our eyes find each other again.

My chest squeezes harder.

"Milaye," he says my name softly, and I don't know why, but it makes the hurt worse. "Why?"

I shake my head.

"Why?" he demands, his voice getting rougher.

"My family... My mother only ever bore females, and her mother before that. When my sisters and I were born, the elders decided that they could not take any chances by pairing one of us to the last-born male of the coastal tribes. They chose a female from a lineage that had males in their recent ancestry. That, and she, being one of the youngest in the tribe, is closer in age to the male. The pairing made sense." I see confusion etch across Drazak's expression. "My sisters and I were raised knowing we would never mate."

"I do not understand? There are no other males?"

Does he not know? Does he even know about the red comet? I can't believe he would not know. "Male children are very rare. They're rarer with every generation," I tell him. "For nearly thirty years, my tribe and our neighbors at Shell Rock have only had one male child, Leith. Just one, in thirty years, the lowest birth rate our tribes have ever suffered, and the northern tribes are not faring any better. The chance of me being chosen for the honor of Leith's mate was slim to none. His chosen mate is also six years younger than me. I had fewer childbearing years to give."

"Why not have him take multiple mates? I have seen other species have multiple partners. Dragonkind only mate for a time, long enough to bring forth young. We do not mate for life... unless a human binds us," he adds.

"Other tribes have their males take harems." I swallow. I remember arguing that very point in the past, before I knew better. "I had asked the elders to allow me the opportunity to lay with Leith, even if he was to be mated to another, so I may have a child—"

Drazak growls.

"—but I was refused, like I knew I would be. They were right to refuse me. Pure bloodlines are imperative among the coastal tribes. They would not risk letting me be an exception, knowing other females of my tribe would want to do the same thing. If Delina—Leith's mate—dies, then he may take another of his choosing, but until then he will remain Delina's and Delina's alone."

"I would not like to share you," Drazak's voice lowers. "I am glad you were not chosen."

His words sting as much as they give me pleasure.

"You are mine, human, mine. You may have not touched me willingly—*if* you are to be believed—but you have touched me nevertheless, and that makes you mine."

"I did want to touch you," I tell him. "Desperately. I was... I was also afraid."

His lips twitch. "I instill fear in all," he boasts. "But I will not have you be afraid of me, not anymore."

"I'm not."

His hand which had fallen onto my lap, comes up again, and this time cups my cheek. His clawed thumb softly grazes my lips. My mouth parts. He's so close that his body heat envelops me.

"You will never be afraid of me," he states.

I inhale. "I won't be." My want for him grows desperate. I feel myself becoming wet between my thighs.

"You will bow down to me."

My brow furrows. "What?"

"As your male, you will allow me to protect you, human. I am healing fast now, and it will not be long until you are taken care of, until we mate."

The butterflies in my stomach vanish. "I can protect myself, Drazak. Very well, in fact." I push his hand off my face.

"You have hurt yourself, and that cannot happen again."

My eyes narrow. "I have been hurt in the past and will be hurt again in the future. I can still protect myself—and you. I am a Protector of the Mermaid Coast. It is my honor and duty."

"Now it will be mine." He reaches for me again. "And I will give you the child you seek."

I move away. I don't want him to touch me. My body aches for him, but... "It is not a negotiation. I am more than capable of protecting myself, and others too. I even train—"

"Not anymore, human."

"My name is Milaye," I snap. A spike of pain shoots through my head. I palm the back of it.

A rumbling growl fills my ears. Drazak tries to grab me, but I get up and move to the fire and out of his reach. Darkness flashes in his expression, and my throat constricts.

I bend down and find my dagger, sheathing it.

"Milaye," he says, deep and raspy. The sound does things to my body, and I nearly go back to him.

Instead, I dig my heels into the ground. "I need to find us more roots to burn. The fire moss will keep these going for a bit longer but not forever. Eat." I nod at the ration he's dropped. I grab mine and bite into it, hoping it'll take away my arousal. It doesn't. "It'll help you regain your strength."

"Milaye, it is dangerous. I will join you." Drazak presses his hand to the boulder and tries to rise, but slides back down. An annoyed snarl tugs his lips, and his tails curl.

Good.

I stuff the rest of my ration into my mouth and move to his side, but not before taking a half-burned root from the fire. I put it beside him. "One thing you should know, dragon, is that I am a huntress, a good one. I may be a human, but I have survived this world like you have. I may want to be a mother, but I will not lose what else I am in the process. It's your turn to rest. You can use the torch as a weapon if you need, but I'll be back soon."

I shift back. He grabs my hand. "There's a naga lurking, be careful," he says. I can see this omission takes a lot out of him. There's frustration and something else in his eyes...

He knows I'm going to leave and there's nothing he can do to stop me.

He stares at me with such intensity it nearly roots me to the spot.

Some of the butterflies return to my belly.

"I will," I say, swallowing.

Drazak squeezes my hand and then lets go.

11

——————

WILL HE SEE ME?

So the naga is here in the cave. I grab my still-burning torch and head back into the darkness. He hasn't attacked yet, and may not attack at all, but I remain vigilant anyway.

Maybe he knows a way out of here...

I scan the darkness. *How would I even ask him if he did?* Humans and nagas speak different languages, if the noise a naga makes could be considered a language at all. I've encountered enough of them to know they hiss in different tones to communicate, but that was it.

And even if the naga did know a way out, and even if we could communicate, I'd have to find him first.

I rub my fingers together, the place where Drazak squeezed them.

His touch lingers. His warmth. My fingers twitch, and my hand opens and closes as the sensation of him spreads. Like the bond, it fills me, comforting me. Each step away becomes more difficult. All I want is to return to his side and be within his presence.

I want to press up against him and absorb all that he is. I shudder thinking about it. I've never felt like this before.

But if he's going to try and take my honor...

I inhale sharply. *I've earned my title.* I will not give it up unless I absolutely have to, and nothing Drazak says could change that. I'm not some little girl unable to throw her spear or set up a cockatrice trap or impale a sand shark. It's been years since I had one of the elder huntresses with me checking if I could survive out in the wild.

I'm that elder huntress now. I watch over and keep our younger huntresses safe. I take the jobs that the eldest of our huntresses no longer can.

I may have thirty-two years, but that does not mean I don't have another thirty-two left to be what I am. And as long as I'm not maimed, my next thirty-two years will be full of dangerous adventures—always for Sand's Hunters.

Always for my sisters, my people.

Haime's face appears in my head. *Has she made it back to the tribe? Is she safe? Is she...* My thoughts shift back to the cave-in, and I shiver. I can't think about it. If I do, I may lose my remaining strength and wither. The loss of Haime would be my biggest failure.

Then I would lose my honor. I wouldn't have any left to give to Drazak. I'd never recover if I lost her. My chest constricts.

I realize my feet are taking me in the direction of the cave-in. I halt.

No, I need to find kindling for the fire. Losing my only source of light wouldn't be good. I straighten. Fire moss can keep anything burning for days, if there's enough to burn, but the roots don't make good kindling, I think. I frown.

How long have we been down here? There's no way to tell time. I'd been unconscious and asleep for part of it, but for how long? There's no way of knowing. The only thing I'm certain of is that the dried meat ration barely sated me, and my stomach feels as empty as it's ever been.

Right now, I need to push myself until Drazak and I are

safe. I've rested, I don't have the luxury to do so again. At least not so soon. And I don't want Drazak to see me weak or in pain. I know the other dragon men are protective of their mates, but I never really imagined how that would be for me if I ever bonded with one. I'd never really thought about it.

Maybe because I gave up on that hope as well. Everyone else had.

But Drazak seems different from them...

Like he's afraid, afraid I'll go away.

I have to make him understand I won't. But will he trust me? He's been stuck down here for so long I can't even comprehend it. What would that do to his mind? Being alone. In the dark. Without food or companionship. Without having anyone know you're gone or missing? What would that do to any being? Dragon or not?

I force myself not to look his way.

I turn away from the direction of the cave-in and make my way around the cavern. Far to my right and in the distance, I see the fire and Drazak beside it. I know he's watching me. I can feel it.

His eyes burn my skin. He'd be able to see me even without the light from my torch. I'm certain. There's still disbelief that I'm even bonded at all, that I have a male to call my own.

That I have my own dragon. I have always envied Issa and Aida for their virile men.

I've barely had time to process him being mine, so little time has passed since seeing him for the first time, since the taut, sizzling heat in my soul sprang to life and knotted with his. Finding more kindling for the fire was a chore needing done, but it was also an excuse. I need to get away and clear my head. I've never needed someone or something as badly as I need him.

Years of lonely nights wishing for a mate did not prepare

me for this. Years of overhearing the sounds of bonded pairs mating never heated my blood like this.

I want to consume him. Or maybe I want him to consume *me*.

Will he?

He's everything that I imagined. Dark, dizzying, and beautiful—even wicked. I'd never known a human could look wicked, but Drazak does. How is that possible? Drazak resembles a dark, fiendish male that had come from the shadows itself. And hadn't he? I found him in the darkest place I'd ever been, and I swear it isn't smoke coming from the jewel on his brow—it is darkness. Like he creates it.

But will he want me like I want him? He's been erect for as long as I've known him... Is it only because of the strings that bind us, or can he want me for me? Making a male erect... It is a symbol of excitement for the females of my tribe. Even the mermaids love priming the few human males they know.

And Drazak is erect—primed—for me. Because of me.

I'm not the youngest or most beautiful female of my tribe. I'm not even the youngest or most beautiful of my two sisters. I may be a better huntress, but I can't cook, my sewing is atrocious, and my craftwork is wanting. I'm the one sent to gather wild fruit and forage for supplies, not to actually make something with those supplies that betters the tribe.

Will he be ashamed of me if we get out of here and he sees me? Really sees me in comparison to the other females, ones he could have been mated to?

I feel my heart sink.

I want Drazak so badly it hurts. I'm wet and aching for him, but I shouldn't be. It takes effort not to climb onto his lap and have him. My cheeks warm.

I want everything a mate could offer me—to never be alone at night again, to feel whatever tremendous way the other females feel when they're being rutted.

I've never had the sexual training given to the other females —lessons in what to expect to happen after a mating ceremony, but I've heard and seen enough to know. That a male's cock goes into me repeatedly—that there is discomfort and a lot of pleasure during it—that there is an intense burst of bliss. A bliss that couldn't be had solely by rubbing your fingers between your legs in the middle of the night.

I wipe my arm across my brow. I'm clenching just thinking about Drazak filling that spot between my legs. The ones my fingers have only dared enter a couple times before, and only out of curiosity.

But will he still want me once he knows there are others, more worthier females?

My heart quakes. I don't know why I'm worrying about it so much.

It doesn't feel right. That I have lucked into this bond when others have died for it...

I will have to prove that *I am* worthy of it.

I glance to the right and behind me toward where the fire should be—but I no longer see it. It gives me a moment of panic. Then I find a distant glow dancing behind some large rocks, one that's barely perceptible. But it *is* there and he is safe.

Moving full circle, I scan my surroundings, realizing I'm much further into the cavern than I have been before. Checking my weapon, I place my back to the fire's light, and continue, keeping an eye on the ground for kindling.

The cave around me slowly changes. Each step is chillier than the last. The coastal tribes only have a short cold season, so we rarely wear our shawls and high sandals, but right now, I wish I had them. Being cold is not something I'm used to.

Something moves in the corner of my eyes, and I twist toward it, stilling, as I watch a long centiworm scurry across the ground. A small shriek escapes. The worm vanishes into the dark. I shake out my body in disgust.

Waters, I hope Drazak didn't hear. I shake again and continue forward, now watching the ground more diligently. The ground is now dirt and roots, differing from the rocks and slate near the fire. There'll be more critters here. The soles of my sandals sink in the softer ground.

The wall I follow turns inward toward me, ending in a bend. The ceiling has lowered and it's right above my head now. I press my palm to it, moving forward. In a few steps, I have to hunker so I don't brush the rocks above.

I'm crouching when I see the edges of rootlike shapes appear. A pile of them. Thrusting my torch toward the roots, my brow furrows.

Dirty and pale, brown and gray, I realize what I've found aren't roots at all, but bones. Bones in an array of decay. I stop, listening to the sounds of the cave.

The naga's den? Or something else's?

I wave my light closer.

The bones are small, with only a couple unintrusive larger ones. Femurs, thighs, wing shards. Most look like bird bones with a couple of cockatrice mixed in. Maybe some reptilians. There are several spines I'm certain are lizards and one small crocodile skull. Nothing that would pose a threat to a predator, not even a small one.

The naga boy is small. This could be his home.

I pull away and wave my torch about the den to get a better look. There are more bones scattered ahead of me, and I carefully step over them. Deeper in, I see that the cave comes to an abrupt stop. It's also much cleaner back here, even the ground is level and packed tight. There are shadows of things further in.

I crouch even lower to reach them. Stopping once to cautiously peer behind me before I do.

There's a small nest of giant jungle leaves with large sticks walled around them. Dead flowers are weaved into them, probably with scents that repel bugs, as I recognize a few. There are feathers from the birds stuffed among the leaves, as well as poorly shorn hides of small creatures. Thankfully, the hides have mostly dried out, even if they haven't been cured correctly.

It's crude, but it's a naga's nest. A small one. There's only one. The nest is only big enough for one.

He's alone.

I don't know why that makes me sad, but it does. *He was no bigger than Haime, and his upper humanoid body was thin. What happened to his parents? There's no sign of any other creature living here but him.*

Nagas rarely nest this deep in a cave. They preferred the undercrofts of the giant jungle trees, and sometimes, they nest high up in the wider branches. But deep in a cave where they can't easily lure prey or drag kills to their nest? It was strange.

Maybe he feels safer here, I wonder. *If he's alone, he probably is... as long as he keeps the cave entrance hidden.*

Which it probably was before Haime barreled after him.

Beside the nest are clothes and old baskets—stolen from my tribe. I recognize the patterning. I rummage through the pile.

There's shells and broken ropes, frayed bags, and plants. Plants, like the flowers in his nest, they all have medicinal or otherwise aptitudes. There are also some pretty rocks and stones, ones I know my more creative sisters would love to have for their jewelry and armor.

Up against the wall is a long, thick stick with a crudely sharpened end.

He's making a spear?

Other naga's use them, but not often. Most aren't smart enough.

I grab the spear, pull out my dagger, and sharpen the end to a better point. Several minutes later, I place it back against the wall and retreat. It's not much, but it's the least I can do. He hasn't attacked us...

Yet.

I debate taking the spear but shake my head, leaving instead. I wish I'd brought a ration with me.

I'll come back later, I decide. Feed him.

We may need each other yet.

My newfound kindness to the naga surprises me. I hadn't cared before—I'd feared he was with family—but now that I know he is alone...

A short time later, I find the roots I was looking for and hear the boy hissing just beyond my torchlight, having returned from wherever he'd been. I hesitate but he doesn't step into the light so I keep moving. The hissing follows me. I wonder if it'll follow me back to the camp.

He must know I hear him.

If he does follow me, I can offer him that ration. The campfire reappears in the distance.

Drazak suddenly steps in front of me.

I stop, lips parting as I catch my balance, and grab my dagger.

"Human," he growls, glaring at me with such intensity it steals my breath. "You will listen to me now."

12

NOTHING LEFT BUT EMBERS

*M*ILAYE. *Mil-aye. Mil-ay-e.*

I test the strangeness of her name in my mind as I roll it on my tongue. It takes away some of the disgust of her human food, the tang of the cooked meat she has given me. I ate it because she provided it, and I know better than to turn away from something that might speed my recovery.

I prefer my meat raw and fresh. I glower at the burning roots, which are quickly fading out now.

My tongue snaps to the roof of my mouth. *Disgusting.* I hope I am not cursed to eat cooked meat for the rest of my days. I will do it if I must, but I will be fussy about it.

"Milaye," I whisper her name aloud, wanting to hear it.

I enjoy it. The names we dragons give ourselves are rarely songlike. We choose what speaks to us as mighty beings of the land, what would threaten other dragons away—what might compel a femdragon to seek us.

My human's name is not threatening.

She says she is a huntress, and I hear fierceness in her voice, but it does not make me comfortable—not anymore. At first, I was proud. If a human female could bind me, of course she would be a warrior. But now that I am moving again, feeling the tug of this bond, this mate—whatever it is—fear has crept in for her safety. I cannot lose her.

What if this is all a dream? What if she goes away and I lose everything? Again? I could not bear it.

I watch her scout the cavern, following her movements as she makes her way over uneven ground and around rocks. While my gaze trails after her, her body, her curves, I greedily breathe in the last remnants of her scent.

Nectar. Female—human—nectar. It keeps my shaft stiff and aching. It makes my hands curl into fists because all I want is to grab her and throw her under me, to run my nose over her soft flesh and find the scent's source.

Would she have let me, if she found me on top of her?

Watching my human sleep was as comforting as it was painful. I had never wanted to engorge myself on another like I had then. But I could not move. I had this feast of flesh—my mouth salivating for a taste—and I could barely flop to my side and lift my hand. *This blasted poison!* If I could kill that poison dragon all over again, I would.

He has made me a weakling. Hundreds of years as a weakling.

He has made me weak in front of my mate.

My tails thump. The tips of them harden to points. I bare my teeth, hissing between them.

Milaye stops in the distance, and I notice her peer my way before turning back to the shadows.

Come back to me, human. Once she is near, I will grab her and not let her go. I will take hold of her and show her who is the alpha of this union.

It should be me finding fuel for the fire, not her. My jaw ticks. I press my palms into the ground and lift myself, sitting straighter against the boulder.

It will not be long now.

I test my legs, bending my knees. I bring my feet closer to my chest and dig my soles into the ground. Pressing my weight down, I raise my hips off the ground, just for a moment. My tails press into the rocks, giving me more leverage.

My recovery is quickening.

Soon my human will see a strong dragon as her mate, and I will be so ferocious she will forget all about my shame.

I glance in at her direction, but she is no longer in view.

She is gone.

I drop to the ground and search, finding I can move my head.

My heart thunders. No matter where I turn, the glow of her torch has disappeared—her body is gone. *She has vanished out of sight, and I did not even notice.* A growl tears from my throat. I could forgive myself many things, but this? If something were to happen to her?

I try to rise but am unable to. My elbows catch me. I stop to listen for her, for her footsteps, for her breaths.

The cave is silent, deafeningly so, like it has been many of my long years. I do not even hear the hissing of the naga. Am I alone? Again?

To have a female so near, only to lose her?

A shriek fills my ears.

It sounds human.

"Milaye!" I bellow, but my voice does not carry. Worry careens through me, and my vision goes dark. I clutch my chest, sensing our bond. My fear surges, knowing it is not just my fear anymore, but hers too.

She is afraid. My teeth grit. I must go to her. I listen for another shriek, another sound, but there is nothing. A single shriek. Would that be the last noise I ever hear from her?

Using the rock, I palm my way up. My tails balance me. It only takes a minute for me to stand, but it seems like an eternity. Finally, I bear my weight on my two feet for the first time, and the sensation is strange. Gone are my scaled toes and claws. Instead, my feet are soft and sensitive.

Every part of this human body is sensitive. Tingles shoot up my nerves as I rock back and forth. Balance does not come easy, and my muscles spasm. I lock my knees when they buckle. Luckily, I have my tails.

"I am coming, female," I grunt as my hand claws the rock.

I jut out my jaw and shuffle one foot forward. Relieved that I keep myself upright, I lunge it forward with courage.

I topple over, the ground smashing against my knees. I howl, grunt, and snarl. My hands flatten, catching me, and I dig my claws into the rubble, furious. Red fills my vision, a dirty, dark red that blends in with the deep shadows of the cave. I smell my blood.

Prove your worth, you wretched beast. I smash my teeth. My anger grows and bleeds out. I'm furious with my human for making me feel so. Our fire might be dying, but I can see in the dark.

Once my full strength has returned, we will not need light to survive! She will need nothing but me!

One of my claws breaks against the rocks.

Shifting my tails, I brace to stand again. Taking my time, I rise to my full height and steady myself. I grunt in triumph. Keeping one tail behind and the other ahead, I slide my foot forward again. This time I stay upright.

Three slow steps later, my lips twist into a smile. I pull my eyes from the ground and toward the direction where I'd heard my human's screech.

With each step, my confidence grows. My tails swipe the cave floor, and with only the occasional wobble, I make progress.

The firelight fades behind me, and I inhale, searching for my human's scent. Fear has a powerful smell. Catching a whiff, I shift slightly to the left, but there is another familiar smell in the air: the naga's. I thought it was the aroma of the cave—the undergrowth and soil and faint petrichor—but I know now that it is *him* as well.

He has been living in this cave with me for a while, I realize. *He came with the rain.*

The smell of Milaye's fear deepens and my chest constricts, but she is nowhere to be found. Relief and annoyance fill me. *She is not hurt. Wherever she is now, she did not come to harm.* But I hate that she is not here at all.

Where the skies has she gone to? I narrow my eyes and glare into the shadows.

Then I see it, the faint orb of golden firelight. It glints off the dull and dirty rocks in the distance. It is nearing.

The outline of her body appears next as she ascends an incline.

"Milaye," I breathe her name as her features come into view, but she is too far off to hear me. She is carrying a load of roots to her chest, her eyes flicking about as she waves her torch slowly.

I move to the wall. She does not see me. The dark pulls itself toward me and like my old self; it absorbs into my flesh and feeds it. My scales get harder, and my horns bulge. My nostrils flare. She gets closer, not seeing the predator I truly am.

I thrive in darkness. There is nothing like a giant monster with teeth the size of small trees hunting you down in the dark.

Her sweat blooms the air. My shaft tightens and rises, chafing upon the rough cloth tied around me. She is all I know. *My prey.*

Almost upon me now, I ready to strike. *If she thinks she will leave me again...*

Her torchlight glimmers over me, but I consume it, repelling the glow. Her eyes go through me as if I am not there.

One more step, female, and you are mine. She steps into my reach—I grab her.

Her body jerks, the roots falling from her hold as she reaches for her weapon. Her eyes widen in shock, in recognition soon after, but I already hear her blood rushing through her veins.

"Human," I rasp, pulling her to me and knocking her dying torch. It falls to the ground and rolls away, throwing us back into shadow.

"Drazak," she stammers.

I lean into her, swing my tail around, and push her against the cave wall, trapping her there with my body.

"You can move." She is nearly breathless. Her hands come between us, pressing into my chest.

"I can move," I warn. "You will not leave me again." I pull her from the wall so I can look at her and steal her eyes. Now that I am no longer prone on the ground, I discover she is much smaller than me.

This is good. I hear her heart thrumming wildly.

"I didn't leave you," she whispers, finally lifting her chin, meeting my eyes.

I snarl. "Going out of my sight is leaving me, human. You do not know..." I trail off. She does not know how messed up I am from all the years alone... I snarl again.

"Do not know what? That the bond becomes uncomfortable the farther we are away from each other?" She removes one hand from my chest, placing it over hers instead. "You're not the only one bound by invisible strings."

Some of her hair falls into my hand. I wind my fingers through it, luxuriating in its silken feel. "What we have is called a curse for a reason," I say, my voice softening.

She flinches.

"It is a curse," I continue, "because whether you like it or not, this is final. It is the sacrifice for stealing my immortality and might. The red comet has never given something without first taking something away. You and I will be together until one of us dies, and even then... the other will follow."

My human licks her lips, it makes me hungry. I wish I was licking them myself.

"No wonder your kind avoids us," she says with a hush, her eyes lowering. "I should have done more not to... fall upon you. I'm so, so sorry."

She sounds sad? Why does she sound sad? What in the skies is she saying?

I bristle. *So she is unhappy to be with a disgraced creature such as I. Is that it?* Any female would be. My hand grabs her hair and tugs, making her look up at me again. "I am more than what you have seen," I growl. "I will prove as much to you. You. Will. Never. Leave. Me. Again." I do not care if she is saddened by our circumstances; I'm the one with the right to anger here.

She is mine, and that will never change. Not for all the world, my wings, my body.

A glistening drop forms on her lashes and falls down her cheek. I cock my head, studying it, knowing what it is without ever experiencing it, this is a tear. Dragons do not cry. They do not show sadness in such a way.

But I have not had water in so long... and I now find I am thirsty, aching for it on my tongue.

Shaking, I dive in. I lick it from her face but miss. My head falls besides hers as my knees give out. Fury—shame—unlike I have ever known erupts while I fall, sliding down her body, dragging my claws, scraping the wall as I go.

"Drazak?" Her hands come up to catch me.

I roar against her stomach and frighten her away, feeling her body going rigid. I slam my fists into the rock, again and again, needing the pain from their impact.

"Drazak! Stop!"

I do not hear her, pummeling the wall.

The next thing I know, my hands are covered in hot blood,

and Milaye is next to me, trying to lift me up. I push her away. "Do not help me!"

"You're hurt!"

"Skies! I want the pain," I rasp, clenching my fists. If I cannot have her, at least I can have this.

"Don't be ridiculous," she snaps. Her arms come around me again. "Let me get you back to the fire."

"I said *don't!*" A bark leaves my throat. "Leave me."

"No."

"Leave! I will not have you see me like this!"

Suddenly, warmth cups my cheeks, a soft heat that forces my chin up. My human is on her knees in front of me, cupping my face. The faintest of lights halos her face.

For a brief moment, her eyes flash with white light. I blink and her eyes are back to normal.

"I get it," she says. "You're struggling, dragon. We both are. I did not come into this cave thinking this would happen, and you did not..." She shakes her head, and I see her flinch. *Her head still hurts her.* "But we can't let these changes defeat us."

"I have already been defeated."

"Have you? Really? You don't look defeated to me."

I bare my teeth. "What do you know of defeat?"

Her eyes glaze over as she looks towards the darkness. "More than you can know. Haime..." She turns away, her face falling into a look of grave concern.

Haime? She said that when I could not understand her.

Then it occurs to me... *The other human. The other one she was with before I turned.*

Where is the other human?

But before I can ask, she faces me again, the graveness now gone. "In the time I went to collect roots, you've managed to rise and walk—you *trapped* me. If you've done so much in such a short time... Think of what you can do a day from now, or even two. This isn't defeat. This is just the beginning, and beginnings are always the hardest."

"Such wise words from such a young creature." I cannot help being snide. She has offered wisdom I know is true, but they are words I do not want to hear.

"Wise words? Common sense. That's all it is. Now let me help you back to the camp so we can rest—" She starts to brace under me.

"No. I will do it." Though I do not push her away.

I could never willingly push my mate away.

"Are you sure?" she asks, hesitating.

"Collect the kindling." I untangle my arm from hers. "I will make it back myself."

She moves away, and I almost grab her back to me but clench my bloody hands away from her.

"I'll meet you back there... then."

I watch as she quietly collects the fallen roots and gathers them under her arm. She picks up her torch, which is now little more than burning embers. She stares at it for a moment before waving it before her. The light is pitiful, but she takes a cautious step away.

I grab her ankle. "Wait."

She stops.

Pressing my hand to the wall again, I rise. It is easier this time, this new body is becoming more familiar. Once I am standing, I take a moment to steady myself before reaching for her burnt-out torch. I hate that she sees this side of me. But she cannot move around in the dark. She is human.

I will lead her back to safety.

She gives me the torch.

In silence, we head back to the campsite. It is slow going, but she remains with me the whole time, not once complaining. Not once mentioning my weakened state.

When we arrive, it is to find that, like the torch, the fire has nearly died out. Milaye makes her way towards it.

The scent of the naga fills my nose.

"Stop," I order, stiffening. She stills, stiffening as well, glancing back at me.

"Something's been here," she says more than asks.

"Yes, the naga."

"So that's where he's been..."

"You know it?"

"Yes. Well, not really. I found his den when I was searching for kindling. He lives down here. Though, I don't think he means to harm us."

I shake my head. This is vital information. "Perhaps not, or perhaps he is biding his time. Is anything lost?" I ask, nodding to the pile of supplies on the ground.

Milaye takes the torch from me and checks, kneeling. I scan our surroundings. I think I see something shift behind a rock, but it is far away and I cannot be sure...

"My shells are gone."

"Is that all? Are they important?"

"Nothing else has been taken, and no, they're not... Apparently he likes to collect pretty things."

My eyes snap to hers, but she is not looking at me. Instead, she takes an oddly foamy item from a pouch and crushes it over the meager fire. It flares back to life, but doesn't grow until she adds the new roots. Then it blazes, drenching everything in light.

I wince. I do not like light, at least not so much of it, but I do not tell her this. The more light I am in, the more darkness I crave—though the effect is slow, and I can handle it for a while.

But my human is a light bringer.

I will always crave the darkness near her. In all ways...

"You went into his den?" I bark. I dislike this far more than the light.

"I did." She nods, sits back, blinks her eyes away from the flames, and grabs another thick leather pouch, raising it to her mouth. She gulps from it then turns, handing it to me. "It's water. Old water at this point, but it's something."

Moving to her side, I take it, swallowing some down. Heaven. It's delicious and fresh. Old is the last thing I would call it, considering I have not had water in ages.

I take another swallow and scan the area again. "Do not enter a single male's den again," I tell her. "You are mine now."

Her eyes slant. But she hands me a small cloth. "I won't."

"Good," I growl. "What is this?" I ask, peering at the cloth curiously. Humans are curious.

"Something to wipe the blood off your hands."

Once again, she is taking care of me, I realize with a glower. I wipe my hands anyway, satisfied to find the wounds are small and already healing, and toss the cloth into the fire. "Now, you should rest."

"There's—"

"No. I sense you are tired, and unlike you, I am not openly wounded. I will watch over you while my strength rebuilds, as I should have been doing all along." Her face hardens, but it does not last, her tiredness returning too quickly. I hand her back her water pouch. "Finish this. You need it more than I."

"We should save it. We may not get anymore."

"I will not have you go without!" I will force it down her throat if I have to. My frustration can only be pushed so far.

She glares at me as I meet her head-on, and we enter a battle of will. My female is stubborn and wants to be in charge, but that will not happen, not anymore.

Eventually, she sighs and drinks another sip of water, but takes something from one of her pouches first to dab on her tongue. With a huff, she lies down by the fire, facing away from me, her body tense. I am temporarily mesmerized, pulled from my brooding by the glow of the light that falls upon her curves.

And the way her skirt rides up slightly, tempting me with what is waiting underneath. My shaft jerks, more pained now than before. *There, I will dominate. There, I will rule.*

Soon.

I lower myself to the ground and slide the dagger from her belt. She twists back to gaze at me angrily.

"You are right, female, I am not defeated," I say. "But I will take this and remain so. You need it no longer."

"Someday, dragon, you will realize that human women are nothing like the females of your kind. We do not have *alphas.* Take my dagger. You're right. I don't need it."

She turns back around and settles.

And leaves me in silence with my angry thoughts.

13

ALPHA'S CLAIM

ONCE AGAIN, something is tugging on my hair, but this time it hurts.

And I know who it is.

I stiffen. He must be behind me because I'm still facing the fire. I squint my eyes as they adjust, but only a little because the flames are already beginning to die. My throat tightens. *Already?* It frightens me. The fingers in my hair distract me though.

Something cool drenches my head, and I jerk, flinging my hand to protect my wound, but it's caught in a firm grip before it can land on my head. "What're you doing?" I twist to face Drazak.

His dark pupils reflect me and the flames. His scales twinkle a deep purple. "I am cleaning the wound. You will not touch it while I do." He keeps my hand hostage. "Lie back down."

Slowly, I do as he says. Part of me doesn't want to get up anyway. I know I've been sleeping a lot, but I still feel exhausted. I've been hurt before, had long bouts of recovery, but it was nothing like this—like a slow-building sluggishness spreading throughout my body. Maybe it's the cave or the darkness… Maybe it's the bond or the wound. Maybe it's none of those things or all. Regardless, I bring my hands up and rest them under my chin and cheek.

Drazak's fingers return to my hair, combing through it with his claws. Sometimes more water is added, and sometimes there's a spike of pain, more than the usual throbbing, but overall, it's soothing and threatens to lull me back to sleep. For a time, I can forget everything. He doesn't know it, but it's the best gift he could give me.

My skin prickles from his ministrations, and I bring my knees into my body. Pleasure blooms. A sneaky, comforting pleasure right in the core of me. I can feel myself becoming wet, and it only worsens when he runs his nails over the top of my scalp.

I moan into my hand, unable to help myself.

His fingers stop moving, and I could cry from their loss. "Don't stop," I beg.

He goes right back to it. He starts again with my scalp, avoiding my wound, and ventures to the hidden skin behind my ears. He rubs it so softly it almost tickles, before trailing my hairline with the pad of his fingers. The tips of his nails graze my neck several times.

He doesn't know it, but he's stoking a heat within me. The heat I've been denying since I first touched him. I curl my legs harder into me.

His nails leave my neck, and I whimper in protest, but his hands gather my hair, making sure it's loose enough that it doesn't tug where I'm hurt. He undoes the last of my braids and brushes my strands. When I think he's done, when he has piled all my hair up by my head, I force myself to rise.

His hand presses down on my shoulder. "Not yet. I am not done."

My heart thumps. I've never been taken care of like this. It's self-indulgent to allow him to continue. I don't know if I can take much more without melting into a puddle.

But I lie back anyway, remembering how we left things off earlier.

I don't want to argue anymore.

I'm weary. Everything is darkness around me, except him. *I don't know if I could've stayed sane if I was trapped here alone not knowing what happened to...* My fingers twitch.

Drazak gives me hope, and though we have a lot to learn about each other still, he gives me comfort.

Maybe it would be okay if I let him take care of things for a while...

I trust him, I realize. I don't know why, but I'm certain he would never hurt me. Maybe it's the bond, or maybe it's him alone, but my soul recognizes his—as if we've always known each other. Though I'm sure we've only been trapped a handful of days.

His hand leaves my shoulder, the other leaves my hair, and they cup the back of my neck. I stare into the fire hard because his hands don't stay put, they move down my sides, sliding the ties of my shirt off. The cloth sags in my front, and I suck in my stomach, pressing my arms to my chest. His hands skim down my body to slip off my sandals.

I wiggle my toes when they're free.

I trust him. The thought blooms inside me, giving me butterflies.

"What are you doing?" I ask as he tugs on my shirt.

"Feeling you. Feeling what is mine."

My butterflies dance. "Yours..." I murmur.

His hands work themselves under my shirt to spread across my back. "You are soft, human, so very soft. I have never felt such softness before. Dragons... we do not have hands like you do. How much of the world have we missed, not being able to experience such pleasure?"

I don't know. I can't answer him because his hands are kneading into my back and his nails wreak havoc on my skin, grazing lightly. Bowing my mouth into my hands I moan again. I loosen my arms. He pulls the rest of my shirt off.

The top of me is bare to the flames. My nipples are hard when I cover myself.

Will he like me? Will he like the look of me?

I face him when his hands don't fall back on me.

He's got his nose burrowed into my top, his chest expanding with each deep breath. His wicked black eyes meet mine, and I've never needed a male more in my life. I don't need to look down to know his shaft is hard under his covering.

"Drazak," I breathe his name. "I want you."

He holds my gaze. "Show me how I can have you," he says, dropping my shirt. The next moment, he's above me and his arms cage me in.

My heart thrums as my eyes shoot straight to his double horns, cast like fine-tipped spears in the glow of the flames. When I find his face again, he's staring at me as if he's never seen me before.

I lie back on my elbows to peer at him in return. His breathing grows heavy, and it's all I hear.

His heavy breaths.

His heady scent consumes me.

A fierce intensity crosses his face, and I swallow. His eyebrows arch, sharp and devastating, leading to those horns of his, but it's his mouth that steals my gaze. It's parted. His tongue slides out to lick his bottom lip. Oh, waters, how that simple action disarms me. He dips lower, and I fall the rest of the way to the ground, leading him to me.

My head hits the floor a little harder than anticipated, and I flinch, reaching up to cup the back of my head, to cushion it.

Drazak catches my hand. "We should be careful of your wound," his voice rushes over me, concerned and commanding all at once. "You split your head open. I cleaned it as well as I could, but..." He slips his hand behind my head. "Rest on me, Milaye."

I let my head drop upon his hand. It's big and cupped slightly to protect me. "Thank you," I whisper. He's so close now that our noses nearly touch. Our breaths mingle.

Our eyes meet again. "I want us to mate, human."

A lump forms in my throat. "Me too." I barely get the words out.

"I have wanted us to mate since the moment I transformed, since the bond formed. Even though I could not move, could barely speak."

Me too... I lick my lips.

"But," he starts, then his eyes narrow. His mouth twists into a momentary sneer.

Worry tightens my gut. "But?"

"But I do not know how it is done between humans." The sneer on his face morphs, and now I can't tell if it's anger, frustration, or derision.

Either way, his answer relieves me. *It's not that he finds fault in me.*

"A male should know how to mate his female. It is a basic instinct. I know this human root—this prick—between my legs thrusts into you, as is the way for all mammals, but where?"

"Drazak—"

"A femdragon bears herself to her male and opens for him, but a human?" He shifts to the side, and his free hand drops down to cup my sex, pulling up my skirt—making my knees come up and my thighs clasp around his hand in shock. "You are covered here, you have not bared yourself to me, and—"

"Drazak!" I stammer when his fingers curl and press into my opening. "Stop!"

"Why?" he rasps, clearly as affected as I am.

"You've found it," I gasp. His hand nestles against my most

sensitive spot. And with my thighs still holding it in place, I can't help myself—I curl up and push against it. A moan slips from my throat. "You've found where your prick goes." I grip his wrist with both my hands.

His hand leaves the back of my head as I lift to rub myself upon him like a sex-craved banshee. I'm wet, so wet, I realize when his hand—which has stayed gloriously still for my sake —grows slick. My thin shreds of undergarments are soaked.

They've been soaked for days. It's wanton of me to have wanted him so badly.

"Are you okay, human?" he asks because I am literally using his hand to get myself off, practically trying to mate it. "Is this part of mating?"

"Don't move," I beg, jerking my hips. If this were a human male, they would think me possessed. I almost think I am, but I can't help it. Drazak presses his fingers harder against me, and I almost scream, clutching him. My nub is a ball of nerves and my sex won't stop clenching. "I want you," I cry. "I want you inside me. It's not part of mating," I tell him. "I just can't stop!"

Drazak flips me over, and right in that moment, my nerves unravel. My body seizes. Unnatural noises fall from my lips as I find bliss. And through it all, I feel Drazak snarling behind me as he bends my knees under me and tears off my undergarment, exposing me to his view.

"Show me where, human!"

I rock my hips, still riding the sensations I stole, already feeling the need for more.

He's bared me for him. I press one fist to my mouth to quiet my moans, and then reach back and press my finger just above my clenching sex. It's torn away a moment later.

Something thick and hard is pressed to it instead. My body shivers in anticipation. A scream for another release lodges in my throat.

I've never learned sex from the mated elders in my tribe,

but I know what happens. You can't be a huntress without knowing what the animals and beasts do in the wild.

Drazak leans over me as I think this, and I press up against him, wanting his body to cover every inch of me, wanting even more for him to do to me as the creatures in the wild. After all, we're in dangerous terrain and there's nothing civilized about our predicament. I'm not being civilized, at all.

"I will seed you, human, and you will bear my young," Drazak says into my ear.

I push back, urging him to take me. "Yes," I mewl, squeezing my eyes shut, sucking in a breath.

"I will seed you, give my essence to you, and dominate you."

I'm shaking, wiggling, barely able to hear his words.

"I am the alpha in this mating," he hisses.

"Yesss, please, please don't make me wait any longer," I cry. I will agree to anything if it would end this torture. The bliss I stole wasn't enough, it barely took the edge off. "Drazak," I whimper. "Please!"

His shaft penetrates, slickened by my arousal, presses into me. My lips part.

I squeeze around him as he forces me to stretch, to accommodate him. He's huge—I saw him, he's so much bigger than my opening—but I know he'll fit.

He has to fit. How could we mate otherwise?

But as he nudges farther into me, taking up all my space and more, a new cry tears from my throat, this one from pain.

Will he fit?

A deep rumbling groan fills my ears, and Drazak's arm wraps around my middle. I bow as his prick claims a bit more and his arm bands hard, keeping me in place. My fingers curl, my nails scrape dirt, and then they bite into my palms.

I'm about to shout for him to stop—when he thrusts *hard.*

Stars fill my vision, and my body tenses.

Mated. Ripped. Banded. Claimed. Words flutter through my

head. I squeeze around him and I wince, dropping my brow to the backs of my hands.

Is it supposed to be this painful?

Drazak hasn't moved, but his body is as tense as mine.

"Glorious," he breathes.

His body shakes.

Glorious? I squeeze my eyes shut harder.

"Milaye, you feel—" he groans the words "—I do not have the word for it. Glorious. My little mate is heavenly. *Skies!*"

My mouth puckers as beads of sweat form to wet the backs of my hands. I wouldn't call this glorious, but each passing second is better than the one before. The tight pain eases.

"You're inside me," I whisper dumbly, now feeling the sensation behind the pain. I'm staring at nothing, my mind whirling.

"Oh yes, human, I am. I will be inside you always."

Pleasure surges at his claim, and my vision focuses. I arch my back. *'Inside you always.'* I mouth the words, tasting their heady threat with each syllable.

His shaft slips out, and I could scream from its loss, the words already forgotten. Drazak growls and thrusts back in, shunting my hips forward. His legs slap mine.

I shriek, stunned. Scales poke the backs of my thighs.

"I will rut you now," he warns. He pulls out and thrusts again without giving me a moment to adjust.

"Yes," I gasp, feeling the rise of my hysterical need. His body pulls away, his hands grip my hips, and I glance behind me when he pulls out and plunges back into me.

Yes.

He does it again, hard and powerful. "Human!" he roars. It echoes.

"More," I plead, exhaling during his next surge. This time I nearly flatten to the floor before he rises back up, taking my hips with him. My core takes him eagerly, despite the ache of the stretch. "More," I say again, when he pulls back out to topple me over again.

I brace, but even so, I'm not ready. He spears me hard, like he's trying to drive the entirety of himself into me. He doesn't lift me from the floor this time. I wait for him to pull my hips back up but instead he shunts against me, sliding his hips from side to side, and rising up on his arms. My mouth parts as he stretches me even further.

"I'm too small!" I cry when he grinds his hips into circles. Every inch of his prick caresses my core, and there's this spot... "Drazak!" Something inside of me, the spot where he rubs, it threatens to burst.

He grunts and stops his grinding before it does. "You are not, female, you fit me tightly, perfectly. You were made for me." He pulls out and plunges into me, emphasizing his assumption. But he stops sliding his cock back and forth. I inhale.

He must take that as acceptance because he begins to move again, and my body moves with him. Like a fiend, he picks up the pace, we're no longer playing, he ruts me. My knees dig into the dirt. My head falls forward, unable to look back at him while we move this fast. I squeeze my eyes closed and grit my teeth each time he fills me.

I fit him after all. My body blazes with heat.

I'm plastered to the ground, and he's above me like a storm. He covers my body entirely, even his tails capture my ankles. My ears fill with animalistic noises—*his* noises or my noises, I'm not sure. They don't sound human, but dark and frightening. I stare at his clawed hand next to my face. There's smoke. Dark wafts of smoke rising from his body. It's making everything grow dark, eating up the firelight. It slides over and begins to stroke my skin.

I feel it enter between my legs, led into me through him, and I scream, thrashing the floor. My core tightens. It tightens so much that I hear him bellow out. He's saying my name, and I think I'm screaming his. His rutting grows wilder. My legs are spread as wide as they can go.

Every nerve-ending ignites as my mind goes blank. Pulse after pulse of bliss envelop me, strangling me, and I'm writhing between Drazak and the floor. He fights me down, pins me, and an earthshaking roar fills my ears. Gushing heat erupts between us and he stills, trapping me completely. His mouth moves in my hair.

His tongue licks my wound. My bliss bursts again as his saliva touches my skin, as I feel him twitching within.

"Milaye," he grunts.

I'm shaking, speared down, against him.

"Milaye, my little human, my fierce female mate," he says.

My lips part but they close back up as another wave hits. More liquid fire slips between us. He grinds once more into me, and my core clamps even harder to keep him from moving.

Drazak rasps with a bout of soft laughter. "I am your alpha." He laps the back of my head.

I don't deny it. Why would I? *We can both be alphas.* Another shuddering, lighter orgasm courses through me. *I'll just keep that my little secret.*

His hands slide over to cover the tops of mine. He shakes his hips slightly and I moan. I'm stretched to accommodate him now, and I can almost sense his satisfaction.

I huff out when he rises off me. "My human is speechless."

His tails flip me over and he slides out of me. His shaft drops hard and thick onto my thigh. We're wet and slippery, and already I miss him.

I don't have to wait long.

He bends my knees up and kneels between them.

"I'm not speechless," I say. Seed, so much of his seed pours out of me. I try to lower my legs. "I'm—" It's hot and slimy, and is spreading everywhere, slicking my skin.

Drazak stops me from moving as if it's no effort at all.

"I'm..." *He's staring at my sex.* I bite down on my lip. "I'm just —" His eyes narrow, and he grips his shaft, holding both my ankles now with one hand. Determination and excitement etch his face.

He pushes his tip inside me. *A gleeful, pubescent excitement*, I realize.

"Speechless," he finishes for me with a purr, forcing his prick all the way back in.

And for a long while, he convinces me he's the only alpha in this mating.

And that he's more than determined to *always be inside me.*

14

———

I'LL NEVER LEAVE

DRAZAK SEEDS me until I've grown too weary. I've let him have me completely. Afterward, he feeds me one of my rations and forces me to drink the last of our water. With my belly full—and my womb—I fall asleep with him inside me, only to wake up several times with a pump of his seed spurting, filling me up again.

It's not until much later that I'm staring at what's left of our fire that I realize I can see in the dark. That the light from the embers shouldn't be enough to illuminate the cave for me. But illuminated in grays, dusky purples, and deep blues it is. The cave should be pitch black.

I blink several times, but the cave remains.

It's an odd sort of vision, and my depth perception is still hazy. But it's vision all the same.

I lift myself from where I'm gathered in the crook of Drazak's arm to peer around. A pressure rises from my chest as my world opens up.

I've been in stifling darkness for so long, I forgot how large the world is. The shift had happened so slowly, it hadn't even occurred to me it was an illusion. But I see, the cave isn't nearly as big as I imagined.

Carefully, I untangle my legs from Drazak's, and unhooking his tails from where they're curled around my neck and thigh, I move away. His shaft slips out of me, but not before he cums once more with seed. I wince, hating the abrupt loss of him, but still myself, waiting to see if I've awakened him.

He needs sleep. I don't recall him sleeping once in all this time. *It's always been me.* I chew on my lip, trailing my eyes over his face. And just like that, I want him all over again. My cheeks blush as I contemplate climbing atop him.

But he grunts, settles his limbs, and continues to slumber.

I still consider mounting him...eyeing his prone cock, chewing on my lip with more force.

Milaye, let him sleep.

I sigh. I shouldn't mount him again until I find a place where we could both bathe. The dirt from the cave, with our sweat and his seed, has dirtied us both—far more than I would like. I've always strived to be impeccably clean—the clean huntress leaves a scant trail.

I swipe at my skin. I find one of my hair-strings on the ground and, still awed I can even see it, tie my hair back.

There's no pain. I gently press my fingers where my wound should be but discover it's gone. My heart thrums from the gift, knowing it was Drazak's saliva that healed me.

What would kissing him be like? We never stopped or slowed down enough to ease into rutting. Rubbing my cracked lips with my thumb, I debate stealing a kiss from him right now, but stop myself again.

Because today's the day we both leave. I don't know why I decide this, but I seize hold anyhow. *There's nothing holding us back.* I find my clothes and finish dressing. *Staying here any longer will serve no one.* I glance around our haphazard camp.

My gaze goes back to Drazak—I can't stop looking at him.

Like if I were to stop, I'd wake up and discover this was all a dream. *But he's here in front of me now, male and wild, he's intimidating, even in his sleep. If I was hunting him... I'd stay clear.* His dragon form pops into my head, large and mesmerizing. *No.* I'd want to run away but would never succeed.

Perhaps that is what makes a predator different from an apex predator. Running versus knowing there's no point in doing so.

I go to my scattered supplies and gather them into a pile, pushing the thought away. Drazak isn't like the other two dragons I've met. There's an uncivilized way about him.

Even so, I know my tribe will accept him. I don't have to worry like Aida did. The tribe would accept any dragon male after the blessings Zaeyr and Kaos proved to be—they single-handedly stopped our imminent extinction.

My fingers pause, clutching a feather that had fallen from my shirt. *Will Zaeyr accept Drazak?* It was a question I'd never thought to consider.

Back when the comet shone, neither Zaeyr nor Kaos were keen on huntresses searching for others of their kind. Nor were they entirely keen of each other—each preferring their own territory. But they did get along, and when needed, would work together for the sake of all our people. Though at the end, they could always separate, returning to their respective clans.

Bonded with me, Drazak won't have his own dragon man-free tribe to stake his claim. I look back at him, worry gnawing at me.

Zaeyr will accept him. He'll have to.

Because if he doesn't then I can't stay... *We'll have to leave.*

Venture into Venys... Into the unknown where my skills may not be enough against the beasts. I shiver. I'm not frightened of the world, but I never thought I'd ever leave my family, my sisters. And I would leave—I know it without a second thought. I place my hand on my belly. For Drazak, I'd follow him wherever he goes. For all the children we'll someday have.

I drop my hand and wipe it on my dirty skirt, rising to my feet again. *None of that matters if we don't get out of this cave, and soon.*

A distant scattering of rocks pricks my ears. I pivot in that direction. And I pause, startled, as the naga boy stares back at me from behind a boulder. He lingers by the ledge where the cave entrance is. Leaning down slowly, I grab my last ration, all the while keeping my eyes pinned on him.

I'd forgotten all about the naga.

I make my way toward him, holding the ration out before me. As I approach, his features come into view, and my throat tightens. *He's emaciated.* Much more now than he was in the jungle. *He really is alone.* I don't know why this bothers me as much as it does. *He looks no older than Haime, and he's starving. He could've attacked Drazak and I, stolen our food, eaten us too, but he didn't.* It bothers me a lot.

Almost upon him, I offer him the ration. He leans back as if to flee.

"Wait!"

But he pulls himself up the ledge and vanishes into the tunnels beyond.

"Waters," I curse, knowing I can't chase after him. Instead, when I reach the ledge, I place my ration upon it, along with the feather I'm still clutching to.

Hands grab my arms and spin me around. The next moment, I'm facing Drazak.

Nostrils flaring, he growls, "You left."

I grow wet at the sound of his voice.

"The naga," I say as if that answers everything.

"Him again? You are never allowed to leave me."

"I didn't leave."

His hands tighten on my arms. "You can never leave me."

"I would never," I whisper, my brows furrowing.

"If you did leave, I would hunt you down, bind you with rope, and chain you to my side for all eternity."

He's desperate. Scared?

He's afraid of being alone. He's been alone for so long...

What would I do if I were alone for so long? I know I would go mad.

There's a wildness in his eyes.

I reach up and cup his cheeks. "Drazak, I will never leave you," I reassure him. It's the truth. "And I'll do the same to you if you ever left."

He lowers his face to mine and traps me with his gaze. The strain in his jaw eases. "Make it an oath," he demands.

"Never," I swear. And right then I realize, he'll never leave me either. Ever. I won't be alone anymore, neither of us will. I'll never be alone again. I'm now certain he would have chosen me over any other female in my tribe. I can see it in his eyes.

First the darkness lifted in the cave, now a burden rises from my chest. But as I study Drazak, I can tell he'll need convincing every day, all the time, until the lonely cave disappears from his mind. We both will. I'm more than up for the task.

"Say it again," he says.

"Bond or not, I'll make sure you're never alone again." I lean up on my toes and steal my kiss.

My lips press against his as he begins to speak, cutting him short. Soft and swift, I lower to take in his reaction.

Drazak stares at me curiously, even surprised. It's better than his fear. "What was that?" he asks.

"I kissed you," I tell him. "It shows affection. It binds a promise." I lick my lips. "It's part of mating. Or so I've heard," I add.

He pulls me up and presses his lips against mine. Hard. I

groan from the pressure, and he loosens his hold. "Not so rough. Softer," I explain.

This time when he lifts me to him, his mouth finds mine like a whisper. I purse my lips to feel his better, but then he pulls away, tickling me with the briefest touch. I groan again, grab his head, and yank him down. "Like this."

My mouth finds his, and I suck in his lower lip, biting it teasingly. Drazak grunts into me, and our tongues meet when I slide mine across the crease to his mouth.

I taste his saliva and moan, dropping my weight to the wall. He gathers me against him and presses me back, trapping me there. Heat and bitter root flavors my mouth, sweetspice and dew. I grow dizzy, my head lightens. Sucking in his tongue, I swallow him down, needing him inside.

Like he promised he always would be.

His prick rises and hardens between us. My legs climb him to wrap around his waist. Something rubs my buttocks, his tails, only to pull my cheeks apart, opening me as far as my female flesh will go. I think I hear my skirt rip.

He's baring me, once again.

He's baring me, and I love it.

His seed is still dripping out of me.

I'm too distracted to care, sucking and licking on his mouth. He grazes me back—and I clench, hard, growing wetter. The dig of his teeth... I need them everywhere. "Drazak," I breathe his name and my head falls back. "I'll never, ever leave you."

His tongue slides up my cheek until his nose is pressed into my hair. His tails and his hands are pinning me, placing me exactly where he wants. And when his large purple-scaled shaft pushes into me hard, my nails dig into his scalp. *Oh.*

There's no waiting for me to stretch for him this time. He pulls back and slams into me again. A long-winded scream tears from my throat, it's punctuated from his impaling, forcing the sound high and then low. I lock my legs around him and hold on desperately as his thrusting grows wild.

He's furious.

Each shunt teases my inner pleasure spot, each pound batters my nub. Nearly split in two, Drazak shows me how fiercely he'll hold onto me, keeping me right where he likes me most—in his arms.

Mine snake around him, embracing him in return.

Sizzling with heat, my sex begging for release, I wiggle my hips to push my nub onto him, writhing as his prick plays me. Like the huntress I am, the one I must prove I am. I grasp him everywhere when my adrenaline rises, and when he is captured, I bite down on the crook of his neck, felling my prey. My sex clamps, and I scream into him.

Marking him. *Mine.*

His roars fill my ears. His seed fills me next. Our limbs lock, binding us, and together our bodies seize from the violent release.

His hot cum gushes out of me and down my legs as neither of us move, panting. All I can do is let him seed me. It's all I want to do.

I inhale his scent like it's my favorite meal.

And of course, my stomach growls.

Drazak lowers me to the ground, slipping out of me. I hate it. I hate it when his root leaves. I only ever want to be filled. I mumble, annoyed.

"You growled?" he asks, cupping my shoulders with his large hands and leaning me back.

"I'm hungry," I whisper, fussy because he left me empty. Actually, I'm ravenous, suddenly starving. My eyes go to his mouth, wondering if it has something to do with his delicious saliva. "Maybe it's because you made me feel empty," I grumble.

"You need food before I can rut you again. Let us get you some food, for both our desires."

He grabs my hand and tries to lead me back to our camp. I tug. "We need to find a way out of here."

"Why? Are you not empty? It is safer to rut you at our camp. I can forage for nutrition there and keep an eye on you, female."

All I want to do is go back to our camp and have him inside me again, but we will not last long if we do. *And if he means nutrition as in bugs...* "Because we can't survive down here, not long at least."

"Of course we can. And we will. There is plenty down here to sustain us—creatures and roots—and I hear a spring deeper within. This is my den, and you are my female, fully seeded. You will bring our young to term here where I can keep you safe. Then I will seed you again until you are done bearing my young."

His words make me shiver with desire and nervousness. "Humans can't live in the dark. We're not made that way. We're not creatures of darkness. We're creatures of light."

His eyes narrow. "What do you mean?"

"We live in the sun, and eat... more than just bugs. We need warmth and shelter—more than what this offers—and space. We need all of this and more. I like it here, but it will not sustain us. This cave is too cold for us without hides."

"I am a dark creature," he says, and as he does so, I sense darkness rising from the jewel on his brow. Darkness that even I can't see through with my new sight.

"I feast off of the shadows," he continues. "They comfort and heal me. I create darkness in return. Here I can be invisible, I will always have the upper hand. We will find a way."

"We won't. We need to leave."

He growls. "So you will leave me? The blush on your cheeks has not even left, and you have proven to be a liar."

I jerk my hand from his. "I am not a liar. I am being realistic! We must leave and go to my tribe if we want to survive. If we want our children to survive. The jungle is too dangerous for two humans, even if we are lethal!"

"With me there is no danger! I will provide everything. I will take care of you as it should be done."

"You are no longer a dragon! And I am not that kind of female!"

His nostrils flare, and he steps right up to me. I straighten, meeting him head-on. The tension has returned to us tenfold, but not in the way it was before.

"I am what you have touched, what you are bound to, human." His voice is low and menacing. "You are mine. You will defer to me."

I return his scowl. "I won't be yours for long if you keep me here." I push past him and storm to my supplies. I hear him following behind me. I drop down, gathering what I can into the remaining pouches and tie them to my waistband. I see my dagger by the dead fire and take that too.

"Female—"

"Milaye. My name is Milaye," I correct angrily.

"Milaye," his voice remains grave but softens when I rise to face him again. "You swore."

"I did."

His tail wraps around my ankle. "Then let me take care of us."

"I will."

Relief floods his eyes.

"But not here," I say. "I need to get back to my tribe, if possible. I have responsibilities."

"Haime?"

I tense. Hearing her name pummels me with all sorts of unwanted emotions. "Yes." I push past him again and head back to the ledge. "Haime. She's my ward. She... needs me." I hope she needs me, but only the living have needs. I make it to the ledge and turn around. He's right behind me. "You can choose to come with me or not."

"And if I do not?"

I shudder. Just thinking of us splitting apart sends terrible jabs of pain through me. But I can't stay here, and neither can he. *I have to convince him.* I peer up at him and inhale.

"You will," I say, keeping my voice level. "Because I need you and I need this. It's not only about our survival. Now that you're better, I need to return to my tribe, I need that more than anything, and to do so, I need you to come with me."

I watch him studying my face. Finally, he asks, "Why? What is out there that you need more than... than this—us?"

"Haime's my ward," I start, though my chest squeezes. "But there's more to it than that. She's like a daughter to me and..."

"And what?"

It hurts to say it, to even think of voicing this. As if speaking it might make it true. "And I don't know if she got out in time." I wrench my eyes tightly shut. "That's why I need to leave, and I still would, even if you provided everything you say and more. I'll never rest not knowing if I failed. If I failed her."

There, I said it.

And I still don't know if Haime survived or not. I twitch, fearing what I've said, praying there aren't larger forces at work. Ones that aren't on my side.

Drazak sighs. My eyes snap open when his brow comes down to rest on mine. "You madden me."

"I know."

"We will leave."

I exhale. "Thank you."

"Do not thank me, Milaye, Warden of Haime. I will not be good company under the sun."

I embrace him and burrow my face into his chest. His arms and tails wrap around me. "Thank you," I tell him again. After a moment, I pull out of his embrace, there is work to do.

He lifts me and pushes me onto the ledge like I weigh nothing. I rock on my feet, steadying myself as he climbs up behind me. Peering down, I notice the ration and my feather are gone.

"Well, human," he says, rising next to me. "If this is what you need, I will give it to you. I will always give it to you. But you must give me what I need as well."

I know what he needs. "Of course."

I take his hand and lead him into the tunnels.

15

THE WAY OUT

I show him the cave-in—the old entrance where I came in however many days ago—pointing to the dirt and rocks blocking our path.

He sniffs the air thoroughly and tells me there's no blood, old or new, in the air.

It's enough to give me hope.

We don't stay long, backtracking a little to find the other path. The clams have been shifted, some are broken, but I pick up the good ones that remain and stuff them into my fire moss pouch. Together we continue, though he takes the lead.

It is his cave after all. But unlike me, he has to remain hunched over most of the time so his horns don't scrape the ceiling.

"There has to be a way out," I murmur a while later. The tunnel goes on and on. "Maybe we should head back and try digging our way through the old path," I suggest. "It might be our best chance of freedom."

Drazak hums. "I will make us a way out if there is not one. Nothing can hold a dragon, not even the terra of Venys—" He sniffs, harshly. "I smell salty air."

"You do?"

"Yes."

I go quiet as we walk. When I sniff the air, I notice nothing but the musk of soil. I trust him though and do my part to protect our backs.

My instincts as a huntress become essential as the territory around us grows unfamiliar. Our trek is increasingly treacherous, with rocks and steep ledges we could stumble over. At one point we're on our hands and knees crawling so long my skin is scraped up. Drazak stops to lick my wounds when the path opens back up.

Then I hear the wind.

It's faint at first, no more than a whispering whistle. But with each step it grows louder, unmistakable. My heart pounds when the whistle grows increasingly sharp. Like it's caught gusting through a small hole. Excitement causes my steps to quicken, my gaze searching for the source, but Drazak stops me.

"There's an opening. There has to be," I tell him when he doesn't budge. "If there's an opening, there may be a way out. Why have we stopped?"

"I smell the naga."

I still at his words. It makes sense. I saw the boy slip into the tunnels, and so far, there's been no other path but the blocked one. And I'm positive we haven't missed any holes in the rocks or crevices where he could have hidden.

"He is up ahead," Drazak murmurs, peering down the corridor. Following his gaze, I see the path breaks into a mass of stones that leads upward. It's steep. The shrieking wind calms for a moment, and I hear the scuttle of falling stones. They keep falling until a single pebble rolls its way to our feet.

Drazak tenses beside me. And this time, when *he* steps forward, I stall him. "Don't hurt him."

His face turns to me with a sneer. "Why?"

"He's just a boy. He's harmless."

Drazak's nostrils flare. "You care about him? Another male?"

"A child. One who's all alone and possibly stuck here like us."

"Human, those snake beasts are no less monstrous than a dragon. They make fine food, but their jagged spearheads and poison are wicked at puncturing a wing, and in our case, exposed flesh. If he wanted to survive, he should have never made his home in a dragon's den."

"Drazak," I warn. "We aren't hurting him. You aren't hurting him. Even if he attacks us, we'll subdue him but bring him no harm."

He scowls.

I scowl back. "We do not hurt children."

Drazak growls and shakes off my hand. He grumps and scowls at me again. My eyes are narrowed, my lips flat, I'm not backing down.

"Fine," he barks.

"You promise? It's your turn to make me a promise," I add.

More growls. "You use my weakness against me?"

"Yes."

"I promise, human." He stomps forward then sprints up the pile of rocks.

"Drazak!" I yell, rushing after him. By the time I catch up, he's already on the stones, the naga boy underneath him.

A cacophony of shrieks echoes through the cave.

The boy's tail swipes out, and I dodge to the left. With his next swing, it rises, pounding Drazak on the back. Screeches tear from the boy's mouth while grunts come from Drazak's.

"Stop!" I cry, unable to see what's happening.

I don't want either one of them to get hurt.

The boy's tail swipes out again and the tip whips my arm. Pain rushes through me. Slapping my hand on the wound, blood rises under my palm. The naga's noises grow more frantic and high-pitched.

"Waters! Stop!" I scream. My voice booms through the corridor. The wind picks up, howling again. I dodge the boy's next attack and grab at both his and Drazak's arms. Not even my male could convince me to allow this to continue. Thankfully, the naga's flailing comes to a halt when his tail thumps on the rocks. A scattering of stones tumbles down the slope.

For a moment, they're the only noise, but then the naga's ragged panting starts.

"Milaye, move back," Drazak orders.

I swallow, staring. He has the boy pinned tight to the ground. *Drazak's not hurting him. He's just subduing him.* I'm relieved. Horrified but relieved.

But I glimpse terror in the boy's eyes and my brow creases. I kneel next to them.

"I said, move back."

"Let me see him," I say, ignoring his order. "Look at me," I tell the boy, making my voice as calm as ever. I'm anything but calm. "It's me. You know me."

Drazak groans with exasperation and I clasp his bicep in reassurance.

The boy glances my way. His eyes stick to me.

"See? It's me," I say, exhaling. "You have nothing to fear from me." My feather is lodged in the boy's tangled hair. "He won't hurt you," I voice a little sternly between breaths as a warning to Drazak. "Neither of us will."

The boy stares at me.

I frown. I'm certain he doesn't understand what I'm saying, but hopefully he senses my intent. I find no recognition in his eyes. They're blank, except for fear.

Drazak speaks, "I told you. Nagas are nothing more than beasts. Nothing more than meat."

I shake my head. "Beasts don't adorn their hair with feathers," I say, indicating the one in the naga's hair. "They also don't collect shells into piles, steal human supplies, or fashion weapons." I reach my hand between Drazak and the naga to cup the boy's cheek. He flinches.

"Milaye!" Drazak barks. The boy tries to snap at my hand, but I'm braced for it and pull my hand away. Drazak tightens his hold on him, and the boy hisses, snapping again.

"If he hurts you, I will break my promise!"

"He won't," I reassure him, still sounding calmer than I am. I narrow my eyes at the naga, and wait for him to stop snapping. "Look at me." The naga does. My pulse flutters. My lips twitch into a brief smile. "I knew you understood me."

"Coincidence," Drazak rumbles.

"It's not a coincidence! Look at him, Drazak. His chest is that of a human male. His face as well. The young parented by dragon men are part-dragon, part-human. Perhaps somewhere in his ancestry, there is a human in him too." I turn to the boy. "We're going to let you go."

Drazak snarls. "I don't like this."

I continue, "When we do, I need you not to move. Can you do that? Not move?" I ask the naga.

He hisses.

"We don't want to hurt you," I say, caressing his cheek once before pulling my hand away to face Drazak. He's glaring intensely at his prisoner. "Let him go," I tell him.

Slowly, carefully, Drazak does just that. *He didn't fight me.*
Warmth floods my chest.

I hold my breath, my attention returning to the boy. He goes rigid at first, and I brace, waiting for him to try and escape, but his strain eases and he curls his tail against him instead. Drazak rises to his feet, finding solid footing amongst the stones. When he straightens with a growl, the naga slithers to the side and huddles. I swallow the urge to comfort him and go to Drazak instead.

I wrap my arms tightly around him. He holds me in return. Rubbing my cheek against the scales on his chest, we both calm.

Though I know his eyes are still pinned on the naga...

Wind blasts our ears. We release each other to look up, and I see a thin streak of light pierce through the gloom. Little dust motes fly through the air. I blink several times to make sure it's actually sunlight that I'm seeing.

"Drazak," I whisper.

"I know." He releases me.

I leave him behind to climb, hands and knees, the rest of the way up. When I reach the hole, I find it's thin, the gap between the wall of the cave and a boulder. I push my hand through, testing the opening with my hand and arm. Nothing budges. It's too small for any of us to fit through.

I bite down on my tongue, putting a little more pressure on the boulder. It's stuck. Pulling my hand out, I notice something on the rock. Long, thin scratches from where something tried to claw its way out. Dozens of marks. Glancing back at the boy, my belly churns. *He tried to escape.* And from the haggard appearance of him, he's been trying for days.

When he wasn't in the cavern with us... is this where he's been?

My eyes find Drazak and I shift to the side. "I can't move the rock. The opening is behind it."

"Watch him." Drazak cocks his head toward the boy. I nod and climb my way down. Drazak catches me at the bottom with a quick hug. He lifts my dagger from its sheath and hands it to me. "I will move it. Use this if he tries to move." He levels his eyes on me. "I mean it, Milaye."

"I'll use it. I'll protect myself and you."

Drazak glares at the boy once more and then turns to climb the slope. When he gets to the boulder, I see him test the hole as I had. He notices the scratches too.

I turn back to the boy and make my way over to him. He

glares at me warily. I keep my dagger in hand, but show the boy my palm. I kneel beside him.

"Are you alone?" I ask although I know the answer.

No response.

"Did you like the ration—err, food?" I rub my belly for meaning.

His eyes shift down for a second. He hisses.

"I'm glad," I say. "I would like it too if all I had to eat were bugs." A beetle scuttles over a small rock by my feet. I change the subject. "Can I see your hands?"

Silence.

I point to his hand. "Hands," I repeat.

His hands twitch. His nails are cracked—gone. I rub my fingertips, imagining his pain. *Nagas have claws... They use them to defend themselves.* This boy has all but trusted his little life to us. Unless he manages to bite me, he has no other means of defense. He slides his hands under his tail.

I frown but don't push it.

Drazak grunts. I rise and take a few steps away. Drazak's back is to the wall where the hole is, one arm through the crack. He's trying to dislodge the rock. His face is scrunched from the effort. He stops and tries again.

A stream of rocks tumbles down.

"Milaye," he calls down. "I need..." Another grunt.

"My help?"

"Your help," Drazak says.

"Stay back and near the wall," I tell the boy as I start for the top. "If it comes down, it's going to come down fast. Be ready to move."

Once I reach Drazak, I start digging and tossing rocks where they might have lodged under the boulder. Drazak watches me, waiting for my cue before pushing again. I move to safety behind him.

He pushes. The crackle of dirt fills my ears, then more

grunting. He stops. I get back down and start digging at the rocks again. We do this several times, and by the third, the boulder shifts. He pushes harder, putting all his strength behind it.

I suck in my stomach. Drazak grits his teeth, his jaw ticks, and beads of sweat pour down his face. His muscles bulge, smoke pools out of his jewel like it's a waterfall, and the plume of it nearly drowns out the light. It eats at it, making parts of the streak vanish entirely.

I've never seen anything like it. Was it doing the same to the campfire?

The boulder drops, and I'm barely aware of it. Drazak falls to his knees in a huff as it crashes down, grinding the stones beneath, building momentum as it falls. I put my arm under his arm, helping him stand.

Sunlight is bathing us.

We're free.

We're free because of Drazak.

There would be no way I could have moved that boulder by myself, and I realize those scratches could have been mine... In another life.

There is silence as the boulder and other tumbling rocks come to a stop. Silence as we stare into the light. It's painful.

Drazak pulls me into him and presses his face to the top of my head. I hear something move behind me, and Drazak stiffens. I look up just as the naga slithers by, sneaking past us and out of the cave. He disappears into the bright light beyond.

16

DRAZAK'S NEW WORLD

MILAYE TAKES MY HAND, and we leave the cave together. It is not an easy thing to do. The sunlight burns my eyes—hers too, I have noticed—and we are forced to go slow.

Adjusting takes a long time. And strangely, my eyes shift before hers. We pause and she sits on a rock next to me, continuously rubbing her eyes and blinking tears. I watch her curiously.

She is different in the light. All the colors I have not seen in ages return fast and swift, blazing my head with stimuli. I see them for the first time again on Milaye's clothes, her skin, her hair. The jungle goes ignored as I feast on the sight of my mate. *Have I ever seen hair so black? Skin so golden and sun-kissed? And her clothes...* They are adorned with shells and feathers, details I failed to notice before, each a splash of Venys I have long forgotten.

She is radiant.

She grumbles and peeks at me through her fingers. I smell fresh tears.

"It hurts," she whines.

'*Humans don't belong in the dark.*' Her words come back to me. I brush my fingers through a strand of her hair. "It will get better. I can always lick them?" I tease.

"Ugh." She turns away and rubs at her eyes again. "No thank you. Just be on the lookout since, apparently, you can see perfectly," she says with a little annoyance I don't miss.

I peer down at her hair in my hand. *Has her hair always been this long? Has it always been this soft?* I played with it for hours when she slept, but that now seems like an eternity ago.

There are other things I discover as well. Things I do not care for...

My human's skin is marred and dirty. There are bruises and scratches all over her. Even though I have mouthed her much recently, I have failed to cover her everywhere. I will have to remedy that soon. Also, there is a tired, shrunken appearance to her that does not look right. Like she is sickly, wasting away... perhaps starving.

I am hungry, and if I am hungry, she must be famished.

I cannot have this. Seeing her like this—not realizing how bad it was before—I am angry. Angry at myself that I wanted to keep her locked away in my den, a place where she would have surely gotten worse. My hand fists at my side. *I need to fix this.*

Now.

I take in my surroundings. Trees rise up all around us, large and blindingly green. Vines hang like unfallen tears, and above, I find that I do not see the sky, not entirely. Whatever sunlight that reaches us comes through a maze of branches. Flowers are sprouting from trunks, and colorful critters flying throughout. I do not recognize anything. Even the trees...

Everything has changed since I last flew through these lands.

Or perhaps it is the perspective.

Noises bombard my ears, coming from every direction. Smells too. It is almost too much, and I shake my head, trying to rid my senses of the clutter. But when I stop, this new world remains.

I sense animals watching us. I sense their fear—they know what I am, what I *was*. Venys remembers those that rule the land and skies, even if they have not ruled in many years.

Milaye grumbles with annoyance, unaware of my thoughts.

She knows this new world, she is a huntress, my huntress. She will teach me new knowledge to replace what I have lost. But first, she needs to eat, to bathe, to heal.

I stand and scoop her into my arms.

"What are you doing?"

I venture into the jungle. "Making this right."

She falls silent as she settles against me. *My huntress, it is my turn to lead.*

The idea of her leading now and again is growing on me. Though I will always be her alpha. *The* alpha. If humans do not have them, they will now. It is all I know.

We walk for a time, I keep holding her in my embrace, using my tails to clear a path for us. After a time, her eyes open, widening to more than mere slivers.

"You can let me down," she murmurs. "Do you know where we're going?"

I shake my head and continue on.

Because I hear water, and I head for that. Through giant leaves, a brook appears. Pink flowers are floating over it. I stop at the edge and dip my tails into it, swiping the flowers aside.

Crystal clear, shallow water opens up to us. Besides some frogs and small fish, nothing hides beneath the flowers. I set my female down and step into the water to make certain that no creatures are lurking, clearing the rest of the flowers out as I do. "It is safe," I say, turning to my mate.

She is already crouching at the edge gulping water from her cupped hands.

I cock my head. *Humans are strange. They do not have long*

tongues to bring water to their mouths—or snouts to take in swallows.

She looks at me over her hands. Rivulets of water slice down her skin and through her fingers. My shaft rises, fills with fresh seed, and starts to ache.

I need her. *Now.*

I stride to her and stand poised. Her gaze falls on my prick. Her throat bobs.

"I need you. We have left the cave like you asked. Now I will claim you for my payment."

Milaye's dark eyes widen, still glistening from her tears adjusting to the light. I tense, liking the way she looks a little too much, liking that her neck strains to meet my gaze so high above hers. I cup her nape. It is warm under my palm.

A human's palm. Not something I ever had as a beast.

I can smell myself all over her. My seed still marks her legs. I see its trails on her calves.

"Now, female," I whisper.

"Milaye," she whispers back, correcting me.

Her obstinance makes me want her more. "Now." I pull her toward me and bring her into the water. She gasps, the sound music to my ears.

"Cold!" She tenses in my hold.

"I will make you warm," I promise her as I lower myself into the water as well. The brook is not that deep, and sitting on our shins, the water only reaches our waists. Gripping her shirt covering, I untie the strings holding it on her.

Milaye catches it and tosses it on the bank. "Yes," she agrees a little breathlessly. Her nipples are hard and pointed, and for the first time, I see the way the colors contrast against her breasts. There is such vibrancy to this world.

I have noticed her staring at me too, now that her sight has returned. Her eyes trailed my face a hundred times. They trailed my chest and shoulders even more. *She is seeing me under sunlight for the first time, as I have her.*

I enjoyed her marveling at my new form.

I feel strong in this body. Strength attracts females. I must be appealing as a male of her kind. At least I hope so. It would make it easier to keep her—and it would deter any other males from stealing her away... Whether those males existed or not... What matters is that I am strong and she is *mine*. Taking her hips into my hands, I want to prove my point.

I pull her onto my lap.

She is sweet and submissive in my grasp, allowing me to move her where I want her. *The submissive female I need.* But then she twists, shifting our orientation, and I enjoy how she pays me for allowing her to take control.

Her legs straddle me as I think this. *What an interesting position.* My shaft falls on her belly between us. She shifts closer, trapping it between our bodies. The view of it against her lithe stomach proves my strength. Pleasure blazes.

It is hard to believe the pleasure I receive from mating her. It is beyond... beyond anything I have experienced. Dragons do not have the means to experience such pleasure. Mating is done only for the sake of younglings. I pity what I was now. I pity it greatly.

Squeezing Milaye's cushiony hips in my hands, I enjoy being a human even more. I glance down at my steely cock. Milaye's hand slips between us. My tip rises above the water, and her palm comes down to greet it, cupping it firmly in her grip. I grit my teeth with a groan.

Divine torture. She squeezes my prick's head and slides her hand down my length. My whole body stiffens, ready to ejaculate everything I have to give. Yet I hold myself back. *My seed belongs in her, not on her chest.* Though the image of the alternative tightens my sacks.

"You kill me," I rasp. Her tight hand slides up, back down.

"Dragon, when you need me, I need you." Her voice is dusky and sweet to my ears. She rises on her knees, still holding my shaft. My grip on her strengthens.

"You are not allowed to leave—" But her body positions over my root and lowers.

"I'm not leaving," she says, sliding down onto me.

I throw my head back, bellowing in ecstasy. I was not expecting her to mount me. I am thrilled, my shaft pulses and widens. Her deep sheath grasps me like it is starving for me, for my seed. She whimpers, and at the sound, my nails bite into her dripping flesh. She tries to rise, but I hold her seated.

Her brow furrows, teeth pressing into her lower lip.

She settles back down, taking me in lovingly.

Her sheath quivers and clenches. With each little movement, my seed threatens to erupt. Desperate for distraction, I caress the ends of my tails up and down her back. I do not want this bliss to end.

"I will always be inside you," I groan, telling her like it is.

I jerk my hips side to side, urging her to widen so my cock may expand with seed.

She twitches and drops her head on my chest. Her eyes squeeze shut. But she takes it. I jerk again, and she cries out.

"So big. Too big!"

"Not for you, sweet human." But I give her time to relax.

When she does, the moment her rigid body loosens, I move. Thrusting my hips up, I hold her on to me. She drops her head back and moans, her soft mounds bouncing slightly. The sight drives me wild.

Pummeling we rut, our tempo increasing, our need building. Neither of us is watching for predators, and the thought of the risk makes my adrenaline race. I almost want something to attack us, almost want to drown in bloodlust just as my mating heat takes over. I can taste it, blood, meat, and rutting all at once.

And with the illusion, my primal dragonhood seizes me.

I slam into her. She holds onto me tight. The higher I thrust up, the more I need her sheath to squeeze me. Crazed, I stand, lifting her with me, rocking back and forth violently. I sense her nearing that moment when she will strangle me, just like I need her too. I hear it in her heightening moans.

Then she does, tightening and constricting my shaft. Darkness rushes through me. My jewel cools, and my thrusting stops. Her body dances on me as I hold her on my prick. Seed shoots out, and I roar.

When I am certain I have scared every animal within a mile of us, I drop back into the water, taking Milaye with me.

She rests against me, shaking.

Pride surges through me because I know, I know that she has finally, completely taken my seed in a way that bears fruit. I feel my body's darkness swirling inside her.

I run my hands up her back and tangle them into her hair. "You are pregnant."

She holds onto me tighter. "Thank you for telling me," she whispers. She pulls back to look at me. "You have given me the greatest gift."

I lean down and place my lips on hers. "And you have given me the same."

I am in no rush to leave, and the light gets brighter in the sky as time passes. She shows me how pleased and excited she is to be carrying my young. I preen at her affection. Her glowing warmth seeps into me, putting my dark crystal to work.

We make the most of the stream and bathe ourselves. I enjoy the newest pleasure of exploring every inch of my female as she lets me take the lead. By the end, there is no place on her body that I have not touched, or have not licked. And I lick thoroughly, especially between her legs. My tongue tastes her at her pure source, where her delicious arousal comes from, and I drink her down. My mate's human nectar is now my favorite flavor.

But I also lick all of her scratches, all of her bruises. Though the bruises are harder to heal, I manage to close her scrapes. When I am done, Milaye is draped half on the bank, half in the water, spread out and watching me with a relaxed softness, an ease that I did not know she possessed. It is a look I like on her.

"Beautiful," I say, climbing on top of her.

She smiles up at me and grasps my larger set of horns. Her legs come around my hips, and I slide back inside her.

By early evening, Milaye is dressing, and there is nothing I can do to stop her. Besides the excursion to find food—where I caught a cockatrice wandering the bank with my hands, snapping its neck to my human's shock—we have rutted and enjoyed each other for most of the day. There was only the small hurdle of how to treat the cockatrice's corpse. Milaye demanded it be cooked by fire, and I insisted we eat it raw.

In the end, my human won.

But she is dressing now, and I would rather have her bare. Always bare for me and my pleasure. I reach for her. She slips away. "I am not done with you, female."

Though I know she is pregnant, my cock still remains full with fresh seed to spend inside her.

"We can't waste any more time. Night will fall soon, and we need to head home. If we're anywhere by the first cave entrance, then we reach my tribe before full dark." She doesn't mention Haime, but I know it is on her mind.

"I am your tribe now, Milaye," I tell her. I need her to know that. "A femdragon does not remain with her nest, when she is grown, she leaves." I sigh, closing my eyes a moment to consider. "But I know that is not what human females do." I do not want her to go back to her tribe, I do not want her to find out whether Haime is okay or not, because if she is not... it would sadden my female, and I do not think I can bear to see her so. But I also know that I will never be able to keep her from going home. Our home, now. I shake my head, open my eyes, and catch her gaze. "We shall make our way there."

The hardness in her face softens. "You will like it there, Drazak. My tribemates are good, strong people." She rips a leaf from the large plant behind her. I follow her out of the water. I take the large leaf she hands me and I wrap it around my middle. The other wrap remains in the cave where I left it. I do not think we will be returning for it.

"All water leads to the Mermaid Sea," she says. "If we follow the creak, it'll lead us to the shore, and from the shore, we follow it home."

Home. Despite my attempts to the contrary, the destination bothers me. I will not like where she lives because she lives near others, despite what she says. I am a lone creature for these past many years, and all I want is Milaye with me, no one or nothing else. I did not choose this piece of me, but a long-dead poison dragon did. I have been alone for so long... even before I fell, life as a healthy dragon is still lonely. And it is all I know. All I thought I would ever know.

She senses this from me but does not know how to respond. *Would I if I were her?*

Part of me wants to grab my mate and steal her away. Take her somewhere far from here. But that will cause much strife between us, and the more I am in her presence, the more I understand I will never control her. I could try to run away with her, but she would never let me get far. My beautiful human needs no one to survive. Even now, she picks out a hefty stick from the low-hanging branches to use as a walker—and a weapon.

I nod when she faces me. I find my own branch.

She is smart to arm herself.

Milaye nods back. She starts to follow the creak. I rumble, moving ahead of her. "I will go first."

She shakes her head and smiles.

Her smile gives me hope. Hope that this new world will accept me into it. If only I can accept it first.

17

NOT AS PLANNED

Something is off about Drazak. His crystal stopped creating smoke. My eyes stray to his back and trace the rigidity of his muscles as we make our way out of the jungle. There's a tightness that wasn't there before...or perhaps I just never noticed the strain while in the cave.

My lips part to ask, but then promptly shut. I know what's wrong. My chest constricts with it, my belly twists.

'A femdragon does not remain with her nest, when she is grown, she leaves.'

I focus on my surroundings instead. My enhanced senses are still odd and colors blast my eyes while sounds from a myriad of creatures sing in my ears. There is no darkness anywhere around us but for a few mild shadows. Night is still a ways off. I love it. I love being in the light again. Little bites from insects itch my skin, and I don't mind, and more scents than I can name bloom the air. I don't know why, but it all seems so new to me. It shouldn't be new; I have been in this jungle all my life.

My gaze drops to Drazak's tense back again. *I can't imagine what this is all like for him.*

What being human is like for him.

How many days were we in the cave? How long ago was it that he could barely move? We escaped the cave near morning. I gathered that from the length of the day so far, but beyond that... the unchanging chilly darkness of the cave obscures time. *We could have been there from anywhere to three to five days.*

I think.

I don't know how long I was unconscious, nor how long I slept. *How long ago was it that Drazak couldn't even move? Could barely speak?* He's only been human for days.

And for me... *I delved into the darkness for Haime. I return to the light mated and... pregnant.* So much has changed.

Glancing down at my flat stomach, a tendril of excitement rushes through me.

Please give me a daughter. I would love a son, but I always dreamed of a daughter. I want both—many—if possible, but I never considered having a son until now. There are so few males that it just never occurred to me that I may be lucky enough to have one. Or given the opportunity to have one.

My heart thrums at the prospect. I'm still reeling from Drazak's announcement that we conceived. I do not doubt him, the other dragon men knew immediately when their mates conceived. I sink my teeth into my lower lip. *He would know too.*

I'm with child.

If I didn't already want to get back to the tribe, I want to sprint there now—even in spite of the ever-present gloom for Haime shadowing over my heart.

But something is wrong with my mate, and I can't shake my worry.

"Drazak," I say softly, reaching out to take his hand. His fingers tangle with mine.

He stops and tilts his face up. "I smell it."

I look at him, confused. "Smell what?"

"The ocean."

He pulls me after him, rushing through the foliage. The run is a relief. Drazak is fast, and the effort distracts me from my concerns. We race, playful as children, and soon, the jungle opens up and long grasses take over the ground. Glimpses of turquoise blue appear between the last of the trees. When his feet strike the sand, his body under the direct rays of the sun, Drazak stops. Panting, I gaze at him. His eyes are wide.

His purple scales twinkle like the rarest jewels.

"Beautiful," he whispers, glancing at me after a long moment. "Beautiful like you. I forgot it."

I blush from the compliment. No one has called me beautiful before. "You forgot the ocean?"

"Yes." He hums. "A body of water envisioned in my mind is nothing compared to the real thing. I forgot its color, its song, its vastness. I remember soaring over it until there was no land in sight."

I round my arms around his middle and embrace him. Pressing my face to his back, I wrench my eyes closed. His words sadden me.

"What is wrong, Milaye?" he asks.

"We can take our time. We can take all the time you need," I say.

His arm rounds over mine. "I do not understand?"

"I know there's something wrong. I can feel it." I nuzzle his back. "I shouldn't have pushed you so soon. Not only have you just transformed, but you recently recovered from a sickness I can't comprehend. You may still be recovering."

He turns in my hold and catches my eyes. "I still do not understand. You have not pushed me. I am well now. The poison and its effects are gone... Any time I need now is for selfish reasons. This time, any time with you, it is everything to me."

I lick my lips. "Then why are you unhappy?"

His gaze goes distant, his lips flatten. But it's fleeting, and the Drazak I know is staring back at me soon after. He drops his stick and cups my cheeks. "Unhappiness is not what plagues me. Nor is it poison."

"Then what is?"

"I believe... it is *change*."

My brow furrows but my confusion doesn't last long. He continues.

"Change from what I was to what I am now, from what I believed was my fate, to what possibilities exist now. Everything has changed, and those changes have been good, but..."

"But?"

"But I do not want *this* to change, *us* to change."

My chest squeezes. "It won't—I won't let it. I like this and what we are."

"Though you wish to go back to your tribe? Where there are others?"

"The others will not bother us. They will help us, protect us," I tell him. "That's what tribes do—what a family does."

"I do not need help," he grunts, straightening. "I will protect us."

"You will." I smile. "And they will do so as well... each in their own way." I pull my hand from his grasp, give him back his stick, and step around him towards the ocean. The sun is descending towards the horizon. "They will make our food when all I want to do is to keep you close and in my cot. They will light our hut's fire so our home is warm when we're late from hunting. They will lead me through this pregnancy and take care of us when neither of us can bear to part from our baby. They will make sure we have what we need when we cannot provide it for ourselves, when our need is something they are more suited to provide. You will see. This is also a good change."

He steps up next to me. "And if I do not want any of that? If all I want is you, and our younglings, and nothing else? If I want to take that entire burden and care for us completely?"

"Then we will leave. If this does not suit you, we will find a new home away from them."

"You are willing to do that for me? You will keep your promise, and follow me? Always?"

"Always, Drazak. I'll never leave you."

"Milaye, my huntress, I will never leave you either."

At the sound of my name on his lips without prompting, I am relieved.

Though sadness still lingers in my heart, I can sense a lightness coming from Drazak now. I do not want to leave my tribe nor the honor they bring me, but I will. For Drazak, I will do so gladly. My thoughts before about my honor and retaining it were selfish. There is honor in many things, and in many choices.

I head in the direction of home.

"But you will give the tribe a try?" I ask and, reaching down to remove my sandals, I squeeze the sand between my toes. "And I mean it, if you're not ready, we can find a different place until you are." I can wait for my answers. "What are a few more days when we've already lost so many?"

"No. We will go. I will face this head on."

I glance at him. "Are you sure?"

"Yes, little human. The sooner this business is done, the sooner I will get to have you again. This human cock of mine does not want to give me a break," he grumbles.

I cough. "Be happy you did not find me during the red comet's *heat.*"

"Hrrmm."

We walk in silence for a time, enjoying each other's company during this quiet moment. The sun sinks toward the ocean on my left, while Drazak flanks my right. Only the sounds of the lapping waves follow us as we travel. Birds fly overhead.

It's peaceful. Golden dusky twilight paints the land, and the jungle falls deeper and deeper into shadows. I know this terrain, this area. We are close to home. I take it all in, breathing it in slowly, because what's ahead may not be entirely good.

My tribe probably thinks I'm dead. And Haime?

Are they out searching for me? Us?

And Drazak. *I love him.*

Smoke rises in the distance, we walk around a rocky bend, and in a few yards, the giant rocks rise from the sand and come into view. It is land that long ago broke from the cliffs that led into the jungle, where Sand's Hunters now make their home.

"There it is," I whisper, my belly tightening.

Drazak grunts. "Your tribe is unsafely exposed. Any dragon could come along and rain fire down upon you."

"Dragon's never bother us."

"Except me. What will your people say when they see me?"

I purse my lips. What have I told him about the other dragon men?

I forgot. I didn't mean to forget.

"About that..."

Figures appear on the beach ahead of us, holding spears, stepping out of the jungle. I recognize them immediately. My two sisters, and... Zaeyr. My belly tightens further. I stop and grab Drazak's hand. "You're not the only one," I say.

"What?" Drazak asks.

One of them spots us and stops. The others turn to face us soon after. For a long minute, all we do is stare at each other.

"Milaye?" Ola, my eldest sister shouts. "Milaye! Is that you?"

Drazak tenses beside me.

"It's me!" I shout back, suddenly dreading facing Zaeyr. He

is only soft toward Aida and his children... If Haime didn't make it...

I just realized he may kill me.

He may kill me. My heart thunders.

My sisters run towards us, and I step forward. They cry out and wrap me in their embrace. I hug them back—too absently —all too aware two alpha males about to clash. *Waters!* This is all happening faster than I expected. Two ancient predators are about to meet...

My misgivings are founded.

"A dragon dares approach my female!?" I hear Drazak blare. A roar erupts, and the sound of flesh meeting flesh follows soon after. One of my sisters screams, and I jerk myself out of their embrace.

Drazak is on top of Zaeyr, slicing him with his claws.

"Stop!" I shriek.

Zaeyr flips Drazak over, streaks his nails down Drazak's chest, and bends one of his tails between his hands. There's a cracking. The sound sends dread down my spine, and I dive between them. "Don't hurt each other!"

"Milaye, stay back!" Drazak bellows.

I'm shoved away, a hand shunts against my chest, sending me backwards. I don't know who's. Limbs, tails, everything is flailing, obstructing my view. Ola catches me and helps me rise.

Zaeyr slams his fist into Drazak's face—but Drazak jerks his horns forward at the last second. He spears Zaeyr's hand. A harrowing, deep scream shakes me. My dread skyrockets when blood gushes between them.

"You have to stop! Zaeyr, he's my mate!"

I want to lunge forward, to step in between again, but my sister holds me back. "Don't!" she warns. "You'll get hurt."

"I don't care. Drazak, he's part of my tribe! No!" They're tearing into each other, not even hearing me. I struggle in Ola's grip.

Drazak throws Zaeyr onto the sand as the water dragon pulls his gored hand back. Zaeyr cocks his long, sharp white and blue horns forward.

They stop Drazak before he surges, preventing Zaeyr from spearing him with his own horns. An animalistic, horrid sound emanates from both of them as Drazak rises into a crouch, looking for an opening.

"Drazak, stop!" I implore. "Zaeyr isn't an enemy."

"He approached you!"

"He is already mated!"

Zaeyr growls. "You are rabid, dragon male."

Smoke oozes from Drazak's jewel at the taunt. Zaeyr's eyes go to it. They narrow, and he bares his teeth.

The light around Drazak vanishes. His form wavers. "A male coming near my female is rabid. I will keep her! You have chosen death, snake." He snarls and jabs his horns into Zaeyr's.

Finally, I slip away, tearing out of Ola's hold and pouncing on Drazak's back. He tries to knock me off him, but I hold on.

"Milaye!" he growls, shooting to his feet when he realizes I won't let go willingly. He thrusts us away from Zaeyr's vicinity. "I will keep you!" he yells. "I will destroy him!" He tries to pull me into his arms, but I bring my legs up, wrapping them around his waist. He will not attack Zaeyr with me on him.

"Listen to me. Listen to me! He doesn't want me. He has a mate, like you and me. He is human now too, see? We are not dragons. You are not a dragon anymore, Drazak. He is Haime's father!"

I hear a scream, and Drazak spins around. Aida is running out of the jungle, and to my surprise—my relief—Haime is right behind her. Zaeyr rises and catches Aida in his arms. She lets out a sob that shreds me when she sees Zaeyr's hand.

Drazak is tense under me, and I squeeze him tighter. He backs up, but I know he's confused. Still, his form fades in and out of the darkness he continues to create.

"Milaye!" Haime shouts, seeing me. I want to run to her, to catch her in my arms the way Zaeyr caught Aida, to hold her close. But I'm afraid for Drazak.

"Stay back, little one!" I yell as she makes her way to me.

Zaeyr reaches out and pulls Haime into his arms, tucking her between him and Aida. I'm thankful and sad all at once.

Drazak snarls at Zaeyr, and the other dragon male snarls back.

"See, Drazak?" I lower my voice to his ear. "He has a mate, and children. He wants nothing from you or me."

Drazak remains tense. So very tense.

Everyone is staring at us.

Another dragon male, I get it. They are rare, beautiful, and deadly beyond belief. They are everything to our tribe of females.

Zaeyr's eyes sharpen on us. "You are right. I want nothing from *either* you, and especially a strange male of my kind," he barks.

We have no relationship, but I've trained his daughter. Despite predicting it, his rejection stings.

"I told you we found a dragon, Father!" Haime quips, and I treasure the sound of her voice.

"So you did..." Aida inhales, staring at us, wiping her cheek with the back of her hand. There's awe and something else in her gaze... Concern? Uncertainty? Fear? It worries me.

Drazak's chest rises and falls, his breaths growing rapid. This time, when he tries to tug me into his arms, I drop my legs and let him. It allows me to get between him and my tribe-mates. That barrier might help him also.

"Drazak, please," I whisper, cupping his cheeks to bring his face to mine. "No more fighting."

"You didn't tell me there were others like me," he says, his gaze still locked with Zaeyr's.

"I forgot. I truly forgot."

Drazak's eyes finally find mine. "I will not live with another dragon male," he says.

I can see that now. It was idiotic to hope.

"Nor will I," Zaeyr mutters. "He has proven he cannot hold his ground. I will not have an unknown alpha in my midst, one so near my offspring. My alliance with Kaos tries me enough."

Drazak stiffens.

"We won't stay," I say, placing my hand on his chest and turning toward the others. "We came for Haime." I look at my ward and smile sadly. "To make sure she made it out of the cave—"

"You touched him in a cave with my daughter in it?" Zaeyr snaps.

I flinch. "It was a mistake."

"So, you risked my daughter and yourself. I had hoped that what Haime said wasn't true."

"She risked everything for your youngling," Drazak barks.

"Zaeyr, *this is Milaye*. She would never risk Haime," Aida warns, but Zaeyr speaks over her.

"I do not care! You have found your answers. My daughter is safe. Now you will go."

Aida protests. "Zaeyr! The tribe is her home."

I step forward. "No, Aida. I will go. This is all my fault." I glance back at Drazak. "We weren't going to stay anyway. I just needed to know... know that Haime was safe." The half-lies come easily, but now that I've seen Zaeyr with Drazak, I know this is our best way forward.

But Ola interjects, "How did you get out of the cave? We went to the entrance but it was gone." Her voice grows heavy. "We've been searching for you for days."

"I—we—Drazak and I were hurt. The cave didn't fully collapse, and once we recovered, we found another way out," I tell her.

"Hurt?" Ola asks.

I shake my head, suddenly exhausted. "It's a long story."

"Did the boy make it out?" Haime pulls from her father's grasp.

Aida and Zaeyr turn to their daughter. "What boy?"

"A naga boy." I'm thankful for the change of subject. For good news, at least for Haime. But in the corner of my eye I see the sun hit the horizon line, a reminder of the coming night. "He made it out." I manage another smile for her. "We left the cave together."

Haime smiles back. "Where is he?"

"That's enough," Zaeyr orders. "We all have our answers now, and darkness is near. Haime!" He is stern. "Boy or not, it is time to tell the elders the news."

I turn to Drazak.

"Milaye and—and her dragon will join us," Aida states.

"They will not!" Zaeyr sneers.

"You are not the leader of us. The elders are. And as future matriarch, I will not turn my tribe's sister away before nightfall, not when she has no supplies, has recently gone through a traumatic experience, and is hurt!"

"Female," Zaeyr warns.

"Aida, it's okay—" I begin.

"Enough! We have much to catch up on." She scans me and Drazak from head to toe. "And I know you would never harm Haime. We all know how precarious she is. You will speak to the elders and tell us how you found each other." She waves at us. "And have a cooked meal. A raw meal for you," she says to Drazak. "When you are both rested, tomorrow we will decide what comes next." When she is done, she turns to her mate. "She will need her belongings if she chooses to leave. I will not deny her all that is hers. This is Milaye's home as much as it is ours."

"Come, Haime, let's head home," Ola says and takes

Haime's hand. Aida, my sisters, and Haime start for the tribe. Zaeyr lingers.

I don't know how I feel anymore. I press my brow to Drazak's chest. There are claw marks all over it, and some of his glittering scales are broken. I'm pained all over at seeing him hurt.

"I'm sorry," I say.

"We will not live together," he says. I know he speaks of Zaeyr. "You should have told me."

"It did not cross my mind until right before. Please believe me."

"I believe you."

"Do you want to find a place to camp for the night? There's a cave nearby that is stocked—"

Zaeyr rumbles. "My mate has opened up the tribe's borders to both of you tonight—to him." He snarls again. "You will honor her wishes. It is the least you can do. I sense, Milaye, that you are with child. *His*, I presume?"

He holds up his wounded hand and begins to lick the blood from it, watching us, waiting for my reply.

Drazak growls.

Ignoring Zaeyr, I continue, "We can stay in the cave tonight, and then I will visit the tribe come morning to collect my things, say my goodbyes." What Drazak wants is all that matters to me now. Not what Aida or Zaeyr wants. Not even what the elders want.

Haime is safe.

She is safe.

From this day forward, protecting Drazak and our family is my purpose.

This revelation lifts a burden from my soul. But it is replaced by another. Though at least it's not as heavy nor as frightening as the last. It's inspiring and hot. Like there's a fire in me that was never there before. It bursts and flows, remedying my worries.

"Milaye," he says, "I will not let you face tomorrow's sunlight alone. As long as the wretch does not come near us, we will go to your tribe together." Drazak's voice is cool and surprisingly calm. "She is pregnant," he growls to Zaeyr. "My human has strained herself much these last few days. We will accept your mate's offering of food and rest, as I find is the human's way."

Zaeyr drops his hand and strides away, following after the others. *It's decided.* My eyes grow heavy.

Drazak lifts me in his arms and follows after him. For the first time, I have no idea what my future will bring, only that good things await us. Sand's Hunters or not.

I rest my arm on my belly.

Tonight, I can sleep with Drazak in the safest place I know: my hut. Where there are no bugs. My male will be with me in the home I built for myself, for the family I only daydreamed would come. Now that I am here, I can finally, finally rest. I have never been so tired.

It seems like I've been keeping myself going, and passing my limit, for days. Abruptly. Oddly, my stress vanishes. It's strange but I don't dwell on it. The fire in my chest expands, filling my limbs. Goosebumps rise from my skin. The last rays of the setting sun infuse me.

The fire wants to fill me up like Drazak has filled me. I let it, allowing it to soothe my soul.

I press my lips softly to Drazak's skin.

He grips me a little tighter, and I let myself feel... *good.*

18

———

DRAZAK'S NIGHTMARE

I CANNOT SLEEP.

I pretended for Milaye's sake, but she fell into a slumber once the other humans started the fire. She dozed in my arms on the walk to her tribe, only rousing long enough to eat. I have never seen her relax so willingly but take it as a good sign, she trusts me.

Though I find it odd that she does not want to show me her home, or speak more than a few words to the other humans. Not even the little girl, Haime, can wake her enough to answer her tirade of questions.

Guilt nips at me. *Is it me who she trusts... or is it the other humans?*

I am taking her away from them.

I shake my head. *It is for the best.* I will ensure our nest is near enough that she can visit. *Milaye was right about having younglings...* I do not know how a human gestates, and if it is beyond my ability to help, I want her close to those who have done it before. Seeing Haime, and the other half-dragon children convinced me.

Do human females lay eggs like femdragons? I stare at the crux of my female's thighs. Her sheath is soft enough for the delicacy of eggs, but it is also extraordinarily tight.

My prick bulges at the thought.

Though dragon eggs are hard and not easily broken, humans are not dragons...

For one, they can mate a lot more often with a lot more vigor. I grab my shaft, shifting it so it does not chafe the cloth wrapped around me. I am eager to bare her again, all the way to my root, but I do not have the cruelty in me to rouse her.

I will bare her for rutting when she wakes.

Zaeyr, the other dragon male, pervades my mind. My shaft softens thinking of him. Now that we have met, I sense him, feeling him in the way all alpha dragons sense other alphas nearby.

It is a mechanism to defend our territories—and our hard-won mates—from the theft of others. Rutting Milaye will be risky with Zaeyr around. I am sure of it.

But as the night deepens, and the raucous noises of the other human's outside my mate's hut lessens, I relax. I stoke our fire. One of the humans brings me slabs of raw meat, and I eat my fill, but no one else disturbs us.

Which is good, because I may snap at any time. I have already had to stop myself from lashing out whenever others near. I hear their breaths outside our walls, the crunch of their footsteps. Every sound puts me on edge.

Where are the thick terra walls to keep us safe? Where are the rocks and stones that block out the noise? Milaye's hut is made of wood slats, reeds, and leaves, all under one large jungle tree. Not safe at all.

Not suitable for my mate, nor my younglings... If I were still a full-blooded dragon, I could curl around my human so she might be protected everywhere, but that is no longer an option.

And worst of all, I now sense a second alpha dragon, another besides Zaeyr. I do not know where he is, but he did not make himself known to me when we arrived. And I am certain Zaeyr does not live with another alpha in his midst.

There was a mention of Kaos... I shake my head, pushing the concerns aside. Regardless, the other alpha's presence grows stronger as the night grows longer.

He will be mated too. I am sure of it. With this many females, he would have taken one to rut. Still, I will kill him if he nears my human. I will kill any male who nears her. My hand's clench. A male, a human one named Leith, gave me clothes, but he was smart and fled before I lost control.

My jaw ticks. There are far too many males here for my liking. Even one is too much.

I distract myself by studying Milaye's belongings. It calms me for a time.

Her hut is round, and hides are draped upon every wall, across the floors, and around the firepit. Each from a jungle beast far larger than my human. Her kills bring me pride, but fear as well—any one of these animals could have killed her before she came under my protection.

There are also weapons. Many of them, and I am curious about most of them. There are spears, some with multiple prongs, and others that are stunted. There are daggers made of bones and unidentifiable items carved from rocks or wood. There's a bow—I know it is a bow from the times the humans of old attempted to use them against me when I neared their homes. I pick it up. With these memories, it is strange to hold it in my grasp.

Once I have scrutinized everything in my view, I pull some hides from the walls and begin collecting the weapons within them. *We will bring these with us wherever we go.*

My nostrils flare. There is a strange smell in the air.

Milaye moans. Sweat beads her brow, and her face is creased. My eyes narrow. I go to her side and press my cheek to hers.

Heat. Humid, deep heat rises from her flesh. It is not the heat of her arousal. I sniff her skin and a sickly sweetness fills my nose. The strange scent is coming from her. She moans again, and I lean away to study her.

Is she sick? My chest constricts. I find the plate she ate from and bring it to my nose. It is nothing like the smell from her.

If someone has poisoned her, I will obliterate this village and everyone in it. I will tear this jungle apart and all in my path. Terror would return to these lands, and Venys would fear the dark dragon who lost his mate.

I take a taste. I do not taste poison.

Regardless, something is *wrong.* I take her hand and squeeze it, finding it limp in my grasp. "Milaye?"

No response.

"Milaye?" I say her name louder. Still, no reaction. My stomach churns. "Milaye!" I tangle my hands into her hair and lean over her. "Wake up! Wake up, female!" I gather her in my arms. "Milaye?"

A banging raps on the door, but I do not respond. I press my cheek to my female's instead.

"What's wrong?" someone shouts.

Milaye's breath breezes over my skin, whisperingly light. Moving one of my hands to her chest, I find the beating of her heart. She is alive, but she does not wake. I bring my hand back up to her face. "Milaye? Can you hear me?" I am overcome with dread. "Answer me, human!"

What if? What if she is suffering what I suffered?

My nostrils flare. It cannot be. The poison dragon has long been dead. My human was never bitten. And though we are bonded, it would be impossible for something like poison transferring between us.

Unless...

I jerk away from her.

The banging and yelling from the door grows louder.

My eyes widen in horror. *Unless it was in my saliva and my seed.*

A crash sounds behind me. I twist to see Zaeyr and Aida with several other females of the tribe stand at the door. I growl in warning for them to stay back, but I am thrown away. Zaeyr leaps on top of me, baring his teeth, and I do not fight him. Stunned, I lie there, as limp as my human.

"Kill me," I rasp. "Please."

Zaeyr's brow furrows.

Milaye's tribe mates rush to her side, trying to rouse her as I had.

"What did you do to her?" one of them cries.

My lips part, but nothing comes out.

I poisoned her.

Zaeyr rises and I clench my hands. But before I can taunt him back to me, to end my horrid life, he goes to Milaye's side. I surge up, shoving him away from her.

"Stay away from my female," I roar.

He growls but remains where he is. A female rushes into the hut—his mate, I recognize—and goes to his side. I turn back to Milaye and the others around her. I growl again in warning and, to my surprise, one of them growls back.

The rest are undressing Milaye and splashing her with water. "What's wrong with her?" the one who growled demands. "She's unresponsive."

"Tell us! Was she bitten by something? Could it be vine drought?" another asks.

"No, she's not turning green," one of them responds.

"Jungle serpent venom?"

"There's no puncture wounds."

"There's bruises." The female who said it narrows her eyes at me.

I push the women away and grab Milaye's form to my chest. "It is none of those things," I hiss.

"Then what is it?"

"Me... It is me."

19

FIGHTING FIRE

"Milaye, fight it!"

I hear Drazak's voice.

Fight what?

My skin is tight, as if it's been stretched like an animal hide across curing poles. But it's the sensation of being uncomfortably full that stirs my mind. And I am full. It's this fullness that's made my skin taut, I'm sure of it.

Every second that passes, my body grows even fuller, my skin tighter. I want to scream, but my mouth won't open.

Make it stop! Please make it stop!

But I make no noise.

Though something does answer me, I realize it after a moment of anxiety. The lazy, relaxing heat I felt earlier roars to life, spreading through my limbs. The warmth takes away the pressure, easing my flesh to loosen up.

Though I still remain excruciatingly full, and that same heat has only worsened it.

The fire tells me to let it in, to surrender into it, to let it consume me. To let it keep filling me and filling me until I burst. I want to do as it asks... but something in me fights it. Fear. I think I'm afraid.

I don't want to burst open. There will be nothing left of me if I do. I have a mate to live for, a baby to live for... I can't burst. I can't.

Someone takes my hand and raises it to their mouth.

Drazak. My heart thrums. *He's my fire. It's because of him that I'm feeling better.*

I fall back under and sweet, restful oblivion takes me again.

I wake to screams. Wrenching, ear-splitting screams, unlike any I have ever known. There's screaming all around me, on every side. It's coming from within me as well, but so many others.

Why are people screaming?

Pain rips through me, and I lose consciousness.

The third time I wake, I'm being carried. Someone is running and I'm in their arms. Each step sends blazing jolts of lavafire through me.

Drazak. I'm in Drazak's arms. I want to smile, but my mouth falls open instead. Several of my teeth fall out. The pain returns, hot and fast.

"Milaye! Hang on!" Drazak roars.

And then I hear the screams again. This time they're all mine.

20

TO WAKE A DRAGON

I RUSH AWAY from the humans, down the lift, and out onto the beach. Dragon fire rages behind me, but I do not stop. Zaeyr follows, helping me with my precious burden.

Milaye is in my arms, but she is not the Milaye I know.

She was not poisoned. After several days of caring for her with her tribemates, it became clear that what Milaye suffered was not what I had. She did not have poison dragon venom festering inside of her. No, I learned that was not the answer when she grew scales, her skin tore open, and her limbs expanded.

No, she is not sick at all.

She is transforming into a dragon.

The alpha dragon that I felt nearing, the one Zaeyr had felt as well. It was not this Kaos from another tribe; it was Milaye. She is the alpha closing in on us. She is becoming one of us.

A scream rips from her throat, and I tighten my hold. Her back arches, and a loud cracking fills my ears. Zaeyr stops next to me and sets Milaye's tail in the sand beside her.

It burst from her backside just as we decided to leave, because with it, dragon fire began escaping from her lungs. She bathed the ceiling of her hut in flames that seemed to never end, and by the time it did, the tribe was in chaos, and I was covered in blood and soot.

Milaye's screams have been unending since. Her mouth still smolders, the flames returning at random.

"I need to go back," Zaeyr says quickly, rising to his feet. "They will need my help putting out the fire."

"Go." I lay Milaye's convulsing body down.

"I will be back soon."

Milaye writhes and anything else Zaeyr says is lost. He worries for his mate and younglings, and that is an honorable thing to do. Though he laid his hands on Milaye, I do not loathe him as much as before. *He stopped my female's sisters from gutting me.*

He and his bonded, Aida, have offered my mate and me a haven. One for her to transform in, one that contains me while I watch over her.

I pet my human's beautiful hair back.

Milaye's eyes snap open.

"Human?" I grab her to me. Her gaze fixates on mine. Her mouth strains open into a silent scream. Sharp, pointy teeth have replaced her blunt human ones. She coughs and chokes and spits out a fallen tooth.

Fear and pain etch her face. My chest squeezes. I would do anything to take the pain from her.

"Mate," I say as calmly as possible. I am not calm at all.

Tears well in her eyes.

"It is okay," I say.

Her mouth moves but no words come out.

"Let it happen, little human. Do not fight it. Fighting will only make it worse." I wipe away the tears falling down her cheeks. Her head drops back and cracking sounds fill the air again. Something wet and slick pushes against my arm. Laying Milaye on the sand, I discover that a wing burst from her back.

She screams, curling her legs into herself. "Drazak," she whimpers. The sound is meek but I am so relieved that she speaks.

I take her wing and spread it out. It grows and grows. The other pops out with another shriek. Dewy and wet, the wings straighten, shedding a glistening filminess. Stunning white hide appears between the shimmering gold joints. They fold and open, and when they expand again, they are bigger and longer than before.

In awe, I stare at my female's coloring.

It is not like mine at all, it is light itself, borne of sunshine. My throat tightens in wonder. What kind of dragon is my female? If she is not of me?

"Drazak," she groans, tears streaming from her eyes. "It hurts..."

I caress her face. "I know, little femdragon. I would take it from you if I could." I would take the pain a hundred times over and more. "If it pulls you under, let it. I will be here."

Her mouth purses, and she shuts her eyes tightly. I lean in and press my brow to hers, giving her the darkness from my jewel. She opens her eyes.

They are no longer dark, but metallic gold. They shine like the stars at night.

I whisper my lips along her cheek when a burst of air rushes over me. It swirls in ever-quickening gusts, and when I pull back, Milaye is staring at me, her body expanding.

Bright light explodes from within her, and her scream assails the air, morphing into a rumbling, heightening roar. I wince, blinded. Something hot pushes against my side, and I fall back, tumbling over and onto Milaye's wing. It rises under me. Through our bond, chaotic shocks of energy grapple me. It is a power I had long forgotten. A dragon's power.

The birth of an alpha.

Milaye's soul invades mine, taking it over. Her roar grows

louder, stronger, overpowering the cracking of her bones and shredding of her human skin. I peer through my fingers, forcing myself to look though it burns my eyes.

Her human body is gone.

All that remains is her glorious new one. I sit upon my knees. The light fades.

Feathers cover her back, reaching over the tops of her flapping wings. Each wave of them sends my hair flying in the air. Like her wings, her body is pearly white and rimmed with gold, accented with crevasses of amber red veins. She is covered in soft-looking scales from her long neck, down to the tip of her coiling tail. Tufts of gold and dark red feathers sprout out the end of it.

Where I have two arrow-pointed tails, Milaye has the power of one. I long to curl mine with hers.

Her dragon is lovely and soft, and everything that would make a male alpha dragon envious and desperate to bear young with her. I stand, covetous, ready to defend my right to be with her.

Milaye turns to me. Her golden eyes enrapture mine, and love explodes my heart. I am torn asunder by the mere sight of her.

"Mate," I say in reverence. "You let me in."

"Mate," she rumbles back, speaking in my ancient dragon tongue.

Pride swells. Excitement builds. She lowers her head, and I lay my hand on her snout. Gold dust sticks to my palms. Rays of golden sunshine streak across her form, and darkness floods from my jewel to eat it up. The light is balanced between us. Never have I heard of a human turning into a dragon.

Never across the lands of Venys has such a show of magic been done.

A dark dragon and a light dragon, two rarities in a large world, finding each other. I clutch my chest, wiping Milaye's gold dust across my coverings. Inside, I feel what I have always longed for. A profound sense of rest.

Ownership, belonging. Darkness and light, and all the suffering I endured to receive such a gift. Power, the power I once wielded over all the lands I claimed. This is the pleasure of soaring over the ocean, of breathing fire. It has all returned to me. Through Milaye.

She stumbled upon me. Touched my dead dragon form. And revived me with her strength. There is human and dragon in both of our souls now.

It makes sense. She is my tough, human huntress. She did not allow an alpha male to do all the protecting. *She just needed to save me first...*

And she needed to wake herself up as well.

Now that she is a dragon, there is no place in all of Venys we cannot go. We need no tribe, no other. Only each other. She and I against the world.

My light bringer. My lips cock into a smile. I am the luckiest male in all of Venys.

Milaye, panting, cants her sleek, feathered head in question at me.

But she is not fully a femdragon yet... The power she now wields is nothing to the greatest dragon gift of all. To experience invincibility.

She has no idea. No idea at all.

But soon she will...

"Fly," I yell.

And I watch her assail the sky, vanishing into the setting sun.

21

HOME

Two Weeks Later

I STOMP THE GROUND, pounding out the jungle soil around the old naga's nest. I have spent the day clearing a path from the cave's entrance to the beach. Not only that but, as to Drazak's instructions, I have claimed the land north of Sand's Hunters, marking it with my pheromones so any animal or beast that dwells here knows who it belongs to.

Me.

Nothing will harm me or mine once the creatures know my scent.

Drazak teaches me more every day how to be a dragon. There is much to learn.

I swing my tail out and snap two jungle bushes in half. Then I crush them into the ground as well. Birds flutter into the sky, and I lift my neck, gazing down the path towards the sea.

"Is it clear?" Drazak asks beside my wing.

I shimmy. *'Yes.'* It's easier to have him read my body's language than to talk in a tongue that twists my mouth.

"Good." His voice is deep and filled with appreciation.

It makes me preen.

He is my male, and he has won the right to rut me. Now that I am a femdragon, it makes perfect sense in my head. When I needily bare myself to him, he just laughs, ordering me to reshape into my human form for that. He runs his hand over my wing and steaks his fingers through my feathers, telling me how beautiful my dragon form is, and that there will be plenty of time to rut later... when I am truly ready.

Which relaxes me because I don't want to release this ball of fire burning within me. Two weeks have passed since I transformed, and I'm afraid if I let the fire go, returning to my human form, that I might not be able to experience this again.

Not only that, but the sun is blissful on my scales.

Besides, I am much more useful as a dragon right now. I can help my sisters and brothers at Sand's Hunters rebuild their huts, the ones I accidentally destroyed. It is much easier to gather wood, to drop them off a tree in this form. I have done it many times now, foraging for other resources in the process. I can access places I couldn't as a human.

Rocks. Reeds. Even mouthfuls of fish. I load my body, carrying everything I can between the other tribes along the Mermaid Coast. Granted, most of the other tribes fled when they saw me, and I've learned to remain away from the villages between trips. But they know me by now.

They know Drazak too.

A new surge of supplies isn't the only change to the tribes my new form has brought.

Not all the changes are good...

There's been a resurgence of huntresses questing for dragons. I told them there were none nearby—I don't sense any but Drazak, Zaeyr, and Kaos—but they would not listen. My words have only led the larger hunting groups to travel farther afield.

I know some will never return.

All I can do is scent my tribe sisters, to keep them safe during their journeys. Each member of Sand's Hunters now wears one of my dragon feathers in their hair for protection. I will not stop them searching for a mate of their own. If they are willing to face danger for the hope of a family, who am I to stop them?

"I have finished clearing the hole," Drazak says.

I twist my neck to the cave entrance.

The tree that once hid the hole from view is partially fallen over. It fell when Drazak turned human, causing the hole to fill up. I ripped out the broken roots, and opened it up enough for Drazak and I to dig. He did most of the digging since I had enough to do: exploring all that is now ours, gathering everything we will need for our new home.

The familiar scent of the cave's cool darkness releases into the air, pulling me from my thoughts, and I am eager to feel it upon my human skin. My nostrils flare. Excitement fills me.

I am desperate to be back in Drazak's arms again. Not everything about being a dragon is great. I cannot be as close to my mate as I want. As I *need*. But will I be able to change again?

Ugh.

At least I am comforted that Drazak remains with me always, that our child is nestled safely inside me.

Drazak wipes his brow.

The smell of his sweat spreads through the air. My wings flutter. I miss having him inside me. Tonight, I want to sleep nestled in his arms, in our cave. Soon it will be a homey den for us and our younglings. I want to journey into it with him. This first time, together.

It is time.

Drazak straightens and steps away from me. Tense, he pins me with his dark eyes. He knows. I see the anticipation on his face.

The need.

I reflect it back to him.

Shaking my sleek frame, I loosen up. I focus on the fire within and imagine it sputtering out, cooling off, becoming smaller. I envision my body fading away. First my wings, my tail, my large, crooked legs. I see my scales drop off, my feathers flying in the breeze, and I feel an ache as my neck and snout pull in.

The fire dances, becoming a core deep within. As the flame pulls inward, my dragon limbs grow cold. My weight and strength disappear. My head spins. I implode.

I black out.

When I reawaken sometime later, I'm being carried. I open my eyes, and darkness meets them. The rich scent infuses me. Drazak's delicious smell fills me too. I curl my arms around his neck. His hold on me tightens.

I'm naked in his embrace.

"I'm human again," I say aloud, curling my toes.

He laughs. I love the sound. "Yes," he agrees.

He lowers to the ground and I peer out curiously, seeing the ledge beneath us. He slips us over it without ever losing his grip on me. When he straightens again, I press my face into his neck.

Then we're at our *'camp'* and a feeling of nostalgia zips through me. The dark is not as dark anymore. I can see through it, even lighten it some with what I am now. Lightness. Though I have no jewel like Drazak. The aroma of charred root and wood, even fire moss still threads through the chilly air, welcoming us. Drazak lowers my feet and I stand. He lays out a thick hide onto the ground which he had draped over his arm.

"Wait here," he says when he is done.

"Okay." I allow him to leave because there is no way he'll be gone long. I listen to his quick steps fade. Our bond pulls tight and uncomfortable, and I inhale from the pressure. I shake out my limbs and busy myself with positioning the hide and looking around.

The cave is as it was several weeks ago. Nothing has disturbed it since, not even the naga boy.

The naga boy... I have not seen him since the day we escaped together.

Though he remains nearby. I can sense him, and when I was a dragon, now and then I would smell his scent. He lives here; he'll be back one day. And when he returns, I'm going to offer him an alliance. I would offer him his den in the back of the cavern, but Drazak would never go for it. An alliance is enough though. Nagas are primal creatures, and living with humans wouldn't be easy for him.

Now and then, I'll leave a gift for him outside. A feather atop my dragon's crown. Protection within my territory.

I hear the crunch of footsteps and turn to see Drazak. His arms and tails are full of some of the supplies we brought with us. There's firewood, baskets filled with fruits and dried meats, more hides, and several spears resting in the crook of his arm. He sets his procurement on the other side of the campfire, taking a grouping of branches after and placing them atop it. I lower and make myself cozy, watching him.

He reaches into a pouch at his waist and pulls out fire moss. I smile as he starts our fire.

"Now you are the light dragon," I tease as the flames rise between us.

His eyes twinkle dark and mischievously. My body warms, making me very aware of my nakedness, of the wetness gathering between my legs, and the scent of arousal coming from the both of us.

"I will be everything for you, light or not. You are my female."

"Milaye," I correct with an arch of my lips.

"Milaye," he says, his voice honeyed and low. My heart quickens.

He pins me with his eyes, prowling toward me from around the fire. The flames dance over his long form and honed muscles, his frighteningly sharp horns. He unties his loincloth and lets it drop. Dripping dragon prick fills my vision. My mouth waters when a droplet of his seed beads at the head of his cock.

"Milaye," he rumbles again, standing over me. My palms drop to either side of me, and I lean back. "Milaye."

His voice saying my name forces a blush to my flesh.

My lips part to say his name back when his tails curl around my ankles and jerk my legs apart. I gasp as he lowers over me, holding me open and prone. I dig my nails into the hide. On his knees, he looks to the wet core of me and licks his lips. My whole body shudders.

I slowly lie back, keeping my eyes on his face.

"I have smelled your arousal for weeks, endured its torture, and have been denied the ability to mount you, my little human, my sweet femdragon. I will not wait any longer," he growls.

His tails spread my legs out a little wider.

His nostrils flare.

"Don't wait," I whisper, clenching.

His hands spread over my inner thighs. He pushes several fingers into me.

I arch back and moan. "Don't wait!" I scream, jerking my hips.

Drazak roars and traps me, pressing forward. His tails force my knees to bend, and his fingers slip out, leaving me dripping. The next moment his prick takes their place and thrusts deep.

My hips rise into the air, into Drazak's pelvis, from the stretch. Two weeks... and my core forgot him. A thrill goes through me at the thought of having to relearn my male again. I try to close my legs around him but his tails keep me taut. He thrusts like a crazed man, and each rough stroke makes me scream.

Each stroke plays my inner flesh, rubbing and ruining my sensitive spot. Deep darkness steals my vision, his darkness pooling over and into me. I grip the hide hard as it bunches under me. Drazak claims me vigorously, harshly, like his two weeks of torture demands aching retribution.

I need it, holding on, tense and open to him. My body jerks with each rough thrust. *This is a dragon's rut. And my femdragon starves for it.*

He says my name again, and my bliss comes hot and fast. I cry out as every nerve ending seizes. I don't know how, but my legs clamp around him. "Drazak!" I shriek.

If his rutting couldn't get more brutal, it does.

He covers every inch of my body, using it to show me how much he craves me—this—and my bliss shocks me with wave after wave of his possession. My body eagerly takes everything he gives. I need him as much as he needs me.

He roars, and hot liquid pools into me. I cry out again as he goes rigid, his thrusts now short and hard, each with more seed. When he's done sometime later, I'm nothing but a sated mass sprawled across the hide.

Drazak lifts up on his elbows and meets my gaze.

He's no longer pumping, but he's still hard inside me.

"I will take you many times tonight," he warns. "Do not think you will be allowed to rest long."

I grin.

We greet the next morning still awake, exhausted and relaxed. Hides are strewn around us, and the fire blazes. Drazak has his back to me as he stokes the flames. Yawning, I watch him, petting one of his tails.

Already, this cave feels like home.

And in the weeks and months after, Drazak proves to me he can provide me anything I could possibly want or need. I do the same for him... when he allows it. Each day our cave becomes a sanctuary. Each inch has been touched by us, and together we take what was once Drazak's prison and turn it into his quiet haven.

Quiet, for his mind. He needs time to adjust, and I want to make sure he has all the time he can get before his youngling comes. He thinks I'll be laying eggs, and I laugh. There'll be a surprise in store when I don't.

The urge to unleash my dragon comes daily, and with each transformation, the shift becomes easier. Drazak and I practice together in hopes that one day he'll be able to shift back too, and we can fly the skies together. I know it will be soon now; I can sense his dragon strengthening in our bond.

Though it is many weeks yet from this night.

"I love you," I say, listening to the crackle of the fire.

Drazak turns to face me. His tail curls around my wrist. "You do?" he asks, hesitantly.

"Yes." I will tell him it every day if it gives him peace of mind. "I love you."

He smiles. I sprawl back and pull him down to me. He captures me against him.

"I can prove it," I tease.

"You can?"

I nod.

"How?" There's a hint of curiosity.

"You've got me tucked away in your cave. You've got me tucked away, and I have no qualms about it, and nor do I wish to leave."

"How is that proof, human?"

"If I didn't love you, I would never settle in such a place," I continue to tease. "I hate bugs. I love you more than I hate bugs. That's proof."

He goes quiet, and I wonder if I said something wrong. I bite my lip.

"Ah, but that is not proof."

My brows furrow. "It's not?"

"No, because you are now part dragon, and dragons all settle in places like this." This time he teases me. "And there are ways to banish bugs."

"It's proof for me." I pout.

Drazak twists to his side to face me. It reminds me of when he first began moving not all that long ago. "I do not need proof." He brings the back of his finger to my cheek. "I feel it," he says.

I curl my hands up at my chest. "I feel it too."

"I love you too, Milaye, my protectress, my huntress of the Mermaid Coast, my beautiful femdragon, and mate. I loved you the moment I heard your voice and I was not sure if it was in my head or not. From the moment I laid my eyes on you in the darkness, and again in the light. I once thought all I had left to look forward to was the smell of petrichor invading my cave, but now there is everything and more. Your silken raven hair, your gold and white scales, your fear of these bugs... I have it all. This feeling is my proof." He places his hand over the ones curled into my chest. "I never want to sleep again. Tonight or ever. I will miss you if I do."

"Then we won't." I smile, rising to push him onto his back and lean over him. "Not tonight at least. Perhaps not tomorrow night either." I press my lips to his.

It is a good feeling, this one we share. This thing between us. It is everything I could have ever wanted, ever desperately pined for, and so much more. Drazak puts his arms around me. Now, I'm finally finding peace in our cave.

I'll never tell him, but I'm thankful he survived for me. That fate—poisonous as it was—bit him and he was here, waiting for me all along. I just had to find him.

Touch him.

And wake us up.

I cup his cheeks and kiss him deeply.

EPILOGUE

One Year Later

I HEAR the snap of a twig and the rustle of leaves. Looking up, eyes squinting, I peer into the brush to my left. There's nothing but foliage, though it's settling from whatever disturbed it. I stare at it for a while in case whatever disturbed it decides to show itself. But nothing does.

Eventually, I turn away and head back home.

Haime is waiting at the entrance, sharpening arrowheads.

I sigh. "Does Aida and Zaeyr know you're here?" I ask, walking up to her and setting down my basket of fruit.

"Has he come back?" She doesn't even look at me. There is only the grating sound of her work.

I glance behind, my gaze returning to the jungle path I just crept out of. "No, he hasn't." I turn back to scold her, "You shouldn't be out in the jungle alone."

Haime shrugs. "Why does it matter? I have your feather with me, I'm safe." She sets a sharpened stone aside. "Can you help me find him?"

"My feather won't protect you from the many beasts that don't care about markings. It won't protect you from tripping or falling, or drowning." She shrugs again, I'm not answering her question. "Besides, finding him isn't the issue, I know exactly where he is."

"Then take me!" She leaps to her feet, finally meets my eyes.

"You know I won't."

He won't be in his den anyway. The naga boy always leaves when Haime is nearby. I don't understand why, and he can't tell me with the few words he knows. My guess is that Haime is a lot to handle, and if he doesn't like her presence, I can't blame him.

"Milaye!" she cries, throwing her sharpening blade to the ground. "I just want to see that he's okay."

"Even if I take you, he won't be there. You know this, seashell. You've tried tracking him, and he has never made himself known to you. And I'm sure he would *if* he wanted to see you."

"You're so mean!"

I sag a little. "I know."

Her chubby face reddens. "You could just force him to show himself with your dragon."

My lips flatten. "You want me to upset him?"

"No!" Haime flings her arms out, growling. "No, don't upset him." She runs past me and down the path. I twist to watch her go, waiting until her little form pivots out of sight as she reaches the beach. Beside me, branches rustle.

"She's gone," I say. "You should go after her."

Iskursu answers with a hiss. The branches dance again, but he slithers away. If I had to guess, he's going to follow her until she's safely back at Sand's Hunters. Which is why I don't think he actually dislikes Haime...

I have a feeling nothing will harm Haime while he's around. Even if she didn't have my marking to protect her, Iskursu will keep her safe. And despite her age, Haime is becoming a fierce huntress in her own right. One day she will outpace me and every female in the tribes along the Mermaid Coast.

That will be a good day.

I crane my neck and glance at the bright noon sun. The light soaks me.

After a moment, I shake my head, pick up my basket of fruit, and walk into the cave. In the past year, the entrance has been widened, the ledge has been reworked into a rockway of stairs, and torches now line the walls. And those same walls have been draped with hides and flowers that dispel bugs.

Most bugs at least.

The other exit is barred off. It's easier to protect one cave opening than two. And in the past year, Drazak found the water source and dug us a pool at the back of the large cavern where we reside. Once I saw how easily it was for his tails to crush rocks and cleave stones, I vowed never to underestimate his strength.

I'm nowhere near as strong as him while I'm human. I can't wait for the day he turns again, when he relearns how, and I can find out who really is the stronger dragon.

I will enjoy being the mightiest one while it lasts. My lips twitch into a smile.

I head for the central fire where he and my daughter rest. Drazak raises his finger to his lips. My daughter is asleep in the basket next to him. I set down my fruit.

My heart warms. I kneel at her side. She coos in her sleep. She has the peakings of both purple and white scales on her neck and hands. I reach into the basket and gently lift her into my arms, hide wrappings and all.

I take my daughter to our cot and lie her down beside me. She stirs but doesn't wake. I curl myself around her.

Drazak walks over and wraps himself around me. I settle into his embrace as I gaze at my little girl.

I've never been happier.

Later, Drazak will chastise me about Iskursu and Haime, but for now...

For now, this is all that matters. I close my eyes and this time, I let Drazak win.

TO WAKE A
DRAGON

AUTHOR'S NOTE

Thank you for reading *To Wake a Dragon*. The last book I plan on writing in the world of Venys. Though there will be a very short piece about Haime and Iskursu later this year! If you liked the story or have a comment, please leave a review. And if you haven't already, keep on going with Tiffany Roberts, Poppy Rhys, and Amanda Milo's amazingly sexy dragon books in the *Venys Needs Men* series.

If you love cyborgs, aliens, anti-heroes, and adventure, follow me on Facebook or through my blog online for information on new releases and updates.

Join my newsletter for the same information.

Naomi Lucas

Turn the page for a sneak peek at Viper, Naga Brides Book 1... A sexy, dystopian SciFi romance with cunning alpha aliens who hunt down their human brides!

VIPER
NAGA BRIDES I
NAOMI LUCAS

VIPER (NAGA BRIDES)

Long have we been alone.

Without brides, without females to warm us during the long nights. Without sweet mates.

But we see them, from afar, brides that could be ours. Kept away from us by walls and weapons. Females we long for greatly.

Obsessively.

Human females.

And the one with red hair? I want her. I saw her first. I will fight to the death for her.

She is MINE.

So, we'll come together and make an exchange with their men that will benefit us all.

After that?

To the winner goes the spoils...

Let the hunt begin.

But the red-headed female is MINE.

Buy Now!

Turn the page for a preview of the first chapter!

ALSO BY NAOMI LUCAS

Naga Brides

Viper

King Cobra

Blue Coral

Death Adder

Boomslang

Cyborg Shifters

Wild Blood

Storm Surge

Shark Bite

Mutt

Ashes and Metal

Chaos Croc

Ursa Major

Dark Hysteria

Wings and Teeth

The Bestial Tribe

Minotaur: Blooded

Minotaur: Prayer

Stranded in the Stars

Last Call

<u>Collector of Souls</u>

<u>Star Navigator</u>

<u>Venys Needs Men</u>

<u>To Touch a Dragon</u>

<u>To Mate a Dragon</u>

<u>To Wake a Dragon</u>

<u>Naga (Haime and Iskursu)</u>

<u>Valos of Sonhadra</u>

<u>Radiant</u>

<u>Standalones</u>

<u>Six Months with Cerberus</u>

<u>Cyber Pool Boy</u>